SCORE

What Reviewers Say About MJ Williamz's Work

Shots Fired

"MJ Williamz, in her first romantic thriller has done an impressive job of building up the tension and suspense. Williamz has a firm grasp of keeping the reader guessing and quickly turning the pages to get to the bottom of the mystery. *Shots Fired* clearly shows the author's ability to spin an engaging tale and is sure to be just the beginning of great things to follow as the author matures."
—*Lambda Literary*

"Williamz tells her story in the voices of Kyla, Echo, and Detective Pat Silverton. She does a great job with the twists and turns of the story, along with the secondary plot. The police procedure is first rate, as are the scenes between Kyla and Echo, as they try to keep their relationship alive through the stress and mistrust."
—*Just About Write*

Forbidden Passions

"*Forbidden Passions* is 192 pages of bodice ripping antebellum erotica not so gently wrapped in the moistest, muskiest pantalets of lesbian horn dog high jinks ever written. While the book is joyfully and unabashedly smut, the love story is well written and the characters are multi-dimensional. ...*Forbidden Passions* is the very model of modern major erotica, but hidden within the sweet swells and trembling clefts of that erotica is a beautiful May–September romance between two wonderful and memorable characters."—*The Rainbow Reader*

Visit us at www.boldstrokesbooks.com

By the Author

Shots Fired

Forbidden Passions

Initiation by Desire

Speakeasy

Escapades

Sheltered Love

Summer Passion

Heartscapes

Love on Liberty

Love Down Under

Complications

Lessons In Desire

Hookin' Up

Score

SCORE

by

MJ Williamz

2018

SCORE

© 2018 By MJ Williamz. All Rights Reserved.

ISBN 13: 978-1-62639-807-8

This Trade Paperback Original Is Published By
Bold Strokes Books, Inc.
P.O. Box 249
Valley Falls, NY 12185

First Edition: March 2018

Credits

Editor: Cindy Cresap
Production Design: Susan Ramundo
Cover Design By Sheri (graphicartist2020@hotmail.com)

Acknowledgments

There are many people I want to thank, but first and foremost, I wish to thank my wife, Laydin, for the unwavering support and love she gives me, not just in my writing, but in every aspect of my life. I also wish to thank Sarah for the endless supply of help and feedback she gives me as my first reader.

I also want to thank Rad, Sandy, Cindy, Stacia, and all the folks at Bold Strokes Books for letting my voice be heard. And for their undying work to make me a better author.

Of course, I thank all of you, the readers, who keep me writing.

And finally, I'd like to acknowledge anyone who is battling or has ever battled an addiction. May you find the strength to overcome.

Dedication

As always, I dedicate this book, and my life,
to Laydin Michaels

Chapter One

R onda Meyers was sore and tired. And bored. She hated fundraisers and the like. She'd put on a good front and done her part. She'd allowed herself to be pawed and prodded like a piece of prime beef. But now she was ready to go home. She searched the room for Gayla, who was in her element, unfortunately. Gayla loved the crowds. She loved to press the flesh. If she could eke out one more dollar of support, she would.

Finally, Ronda spotted Gayla. Their gazes met across the crowded room. Gayla's pleaded for one more minute, just as Ronda's pleaded for them to leave right then. Gayla gave in and crossed the room to where Ronda stood waiting for her.

"Baby." Gayla ran her hand over Ronda's jacket and down her arm. "Things are going great here. Do we have to leave now?"

"You're not the one who had practice today. I'm wiped out. Besides, this isn't your gig. You're not putting it on. So, you've already done enough."

"Still, any penny we can use to raise the awareness of you women, we need to do it. We need fans in those seats. The bigger the American Women's Football Association gets, the more money you get."

"I get that. Believe me. But right now, I'm tired of being one of the poster girls for the sport. I want to get out of here."

They made their way to the Goldens who were throwing this particular fundraiser. They thanked them for their hard work and said their good-byes.

Ronda could feel the tension leaving her body as she sat in their hired car.

"Man, I hate those things," she said.

"You shouldn't. People pay top dollar to come and see you."

It was true. Ronda not only played for the championship team, she was the reigning league MVP. People did pay whatever was asked to rub shoulders with her, feel her biceps, and some even tried to squeeze a hamstring or quad.

That was going too far, and Ronda would have to play it off when all she wanted to do was punch those people in the face. She was a human being, after all, not just a piece of meat.

Ronda opened an eye and looked over at Gayla. She had on a black cocktail dress that was split high enough to show off her shapely thighs. And Gayla had great thighs. She was Ronda's assistant and she worked very hard for her. But occasionally, no, often, they crossed that line from professional to personal. Ronda, exhausted though she was, hoped that night would be one of those times. She crossed over to sit next to Gayla and put her arm around her.

"So, how you doin'? Besides bein' pissed at me for making you leave the gala early?"

"Ah. That was cute. Gayla. Gala. You're a clever one."

"I like to think so," Ronda said. "So, anyway, how you doin'? Are you still pumped from the festivities?"

"I am."

"So, should I have the car drop us off at my place? I'm sure I could find a way to help relax you."

"But you're wiped out."

"I think I feel a second wind coming on."

"What time is practice tomorrow?"

"Ten."

"Okay, then," Gayla said. "We can go back to your place."

She rested her hand on Gayla's thigh and the heat radiated throughout her body. Damn, she was hot. Gayla stood five foot nine in her bare feet, but she was seldom in bare feet. She could normally be found in two- to three-inch heels, which made her almost the same height as Ronda.

She kept her blond hair short. It fell just below her jaw. Her green eyes had just the right amount of makeup on them, whether it was for a meeting or a fundraiser. She knew how to do things right. And then there were her lips. Full and always ready with a smile. Unless Ronda had made some egregious error. Then, there was no smile. Not for a long time. But Ronda did her best to be where she was told to be when she was told to be there, whether it was during the season, or in the off-season, when she was a real estate broker. Gayla took good care of her and she was in the mood to take good care of Gayla.

The car pulled up in front of her house and they climbed out. Ronda slipped the driver a twenty and offered Gayla her elbow. She took it and they strolled up the rock pathway until they came to the porch. It was a wraparound, Southern style porch that Ronda was quite proud of.

"Did you want something to drink?" Ronda asked.

"I'd love a scotch," Gayla said.

"Would you mind sitting out here?"

"Not at all."

"Great. Have a seat and I'll get our drinks."

Ronda came out with two glasses of scotch. She handed one to Gayla then took a seat across from her at the little table set she had on the porch.

"You know, like it or not, you were great tonight," Gayla said.

"Thank you, but you know I hate those things. I feel like a prized bull on display."

"Yes, but you're this town's prized bull and they want to see you and take pictures with you so they can tweet them and Instagram them. You're famous, baby. You have to accept that."

"Can't I be famous far from the madding crowds?"

"Nope. Sorry good lookin' you need to literally press the flesh," Gayla said. "Just pretend you're in a club with all your girls and everyone wants a piece of you. You never seem to mind that."

"That's different."

Gayla laughed, a sound that made Ronda's clit swell. More than once, people had suggested they become an item. Sometimes it seemed like a good idea. But then she thought about nights in the clubs and she knew there was no way she'd ever settle down.

Ronda noticed Gayla's glass was empty.

"You ready to go inside?" she said.

"Sure."

Ronda took Gayla's hand and took her back to the bedroom. She placed her hand behind her neck and pulled her to her.

"You look especially gorgeous tonight," Ronda said.

"Thank you."

Ronda leaned forward and claimed Gayla's lips. The kiss was soft at first, then Ronda ran her tongue along Gayla's lips and Gayla parted them and welcomed Ronda inside. The familiarity of the kiss did little to downplay it. If anything, it made it hotter. New kisses were always fun, but kissing someone when you knew what they liked and knew what was coming next, could also be arousing as hell.

Ronda continued to kiss Gayla as she reached around her and unzipped her dress. She stepped back while Gayla stepped out of it. Gayla could have been an athlete, also, with her fine, trim body. Except her body was soft and smooth, where Ronda's was hard and muscular.

"Damn, woman. You never cease to take my breath away," Ronda said.

She kissed her again and reached around to unhook her bra. She took it off and tossed it to the floor. She brought her hands around to her front and played with her breasts.

"Man, I love these things."

"Good. They love the way you touch them."

Ronda dragged her thumbs over Gayla's nipples and felt them tighten.

"Mm. Let's get you on the bed," Ronda said. She lowered Gayla to the bed and kissed her with a passion that came from deep within her. She kissed down Gayla's cheek and nibbled on her neck. She kissed down her chest and stopped to suck first on one nipple, then the other. Ronda was getting hotter by the minute. She couldn't wait to take Gayla as far as she could go.

She kissed down her soft belly until she was between her legs. "How did we manage to leave these on?" she asked as she fingered the waistband of Gayla's panties.

"I don't know, but please take them off."

"Are you sure? Maybe they don't need to come off just yet."

"Baby, they need to come off. Take them off. Please."

Ronda loved when Gayla begged. Her voice went up an octave, and the sound got Ronda dripping wet. She peeled Gayla's panties off and tossed them to the floor. She gazed at the beauty before her.

"I don't know where to start," she murmured.

"Anywhere. Just fucking start," Gayla said.

Ronda laughed and lowered her mouth to taste Gayla. She licked around her opening before darting her tongue inside. She relished the familiar flavor and ran her tongue all over. She moved to Gayla's clit and sucked it in her mouth. She lapped at it as she sucked. She heard Gayla's breathing getting shallow.

Ronda reached up and pinched a nipple as she licked and sucked. That's all it took. Gayla pressed Ronda's face into her before crying out in ecstasy. Gayla finally released Ronda, who climbed up next to her.

"How is it you're still dressed?" Gayla said.

"I'm not sure how that happened. I guess I was in too much of a hurry to get to you."

"Well, get them off now, because I'm in a hurry to get to you."

"Fair enough."

Ronda took off her suit and carefully laid it over the back of the chair. She undid her cufflinks and shrugged out of her shirt.

"Damn you and your broad shoulders," Gayla said.

Ronda paused and looked at her.

"Keep going," Gayla said.

Ronda took off her sports bra and stepped out of her boxers. She stood naked for Gayla's approval.

"You are so fine," Gayla said. "You're like a sculpted piece of ebony and I can't wait to get at you."

Ronda lay down on the bed next to Gayla. Gayla propped herself up on an elbow and looked down at Ronda.

"Do you know how many women in that room tonight would kill to be me right now?"

"I think most of them were straight, so I doubt this even crossed their minds."

"Then they were fools."

She lowered her head and kissed Ronda on the mouth. She sucked her bottom lip and ran her tongue over it. She kissed her on the mouth again and slid her tongue inside. Ronda grew dizzy from the kiss. Gayla knew how to use her tongue. There was no doubt about that.

Gayla moved her mouth to Ronda's breasts.

"I love your breasts," she said.

"They're not much more than mosquito bites," Ronda said.

"But they go well with the rest of your body."

She sucked a nipple into her mouth and ran her tongue over it. Ronda clutched her head and tangled her hands in Gayla's hair. God, that woman knew what she was doing.

Gayla continued to suck as she ran her hand down Ronda's body until it came to rest between her legs. She stroked Ronda's clit softly before plunging her fingers inside. She rubbed the satin walls until Ronda was writhing on the bed, begging for release. Gayla moved back to her clit and pressed it into Ronda's pubis until Ronda arched off the bed and then collapsed as wave after wave of orgasm cascaded over her.

It took Ronda a moment to catch her breath.

"Damn, woman. You sure know what you're doing

"I should by now. You're easy to please, baby."

Gayla snuggled against Ronda.

"I like it when you wrap your arm around me," Gayla said. "It's so strong, yet comforting at the same time."

Ronda stiffened slightly. She wasn't sure she wanted Gayla getting too comfortable.

"Relax, gorgeous," Gayla said. "I'm not asking you to marry me. Just saying I like cuddling with you after sex. Jeez."

Ronda laughed.

"Sorry. I forget. So many women who share my bed have expectations…"

"I don't, baby. The only expectation I have is that you make it to practice tomorrow. And then I believe you have a house showing in the afternoon, but I'll have to check my calendar for that."

"That's fine, Gayla. Let's not worry about that right now. For now, let's just sleep."

Ronda woke the next morning and looked at the clock. Eight o'clock. She had two hours until practice. She contemplated waking Gayla, but decided she looked too peaceful sleeping there. Instead she went to the kitchen to make her breakfast. She was still on her first cup of coffee when she heard Gayla padding out to join her.

She took in the long lines of Gayla's nude body and was tempted to take her back to bed. But she needed her energy for practice. That sounded so cliché to her, but she knew Gayla would tell her the same thing.

"You should cover up so I don't take you back to bed right now," she said.

"Uh-uh. You need to conserve your energy. And I don't want to cover up. You're not."

"No, I'm not. Maybe we both should."

"Or not. There's nothing wrong with being as nature intended us."

"Fine," Ronda said.

She served them each a plate of bacon and eggs and they sat at the table.

"So, you have a house to show in Upper Kirby at three o'clock. What time is practice over?"

"It's over at one. I'll have plenty of time to make my appointment."

"Good. Then your evening is free."

"Most excellent. I'll enjoy my free time."

"Well, you know, hot stuff, if you want some company…"

"We'll see. Maybe I will. If so, you'll be the first to know."

Chapter Two

Practice was intense, as usual. The Houston Stars were expected to repeat that year, and Coach Hindley was doing everything in her power to get her defense ready for the opening game, which was less than a month away. And she wasn't taking it easy on her star.

"Meyers!" she called to Ronda. "Lift those knees higher. Be lighter on your feet. Come on. We've got games to win."

Ronda went through calisthenics with the rest of the team, doing her best to be the leader she was expected to be. She didn't like being the leader. She just wanted to play football. But she knew she was lying to herself. She loved being the leader. She got first shot at the rookies. She had first choice of the ladies at the clubs. Being the leader had its perks, so she tried to run faster and jump higher and tackle harder.

When she was off the field for a few plays, she kept her focus on the girl who'd just started with the team. She'd been traded from New Orleans. She was a looker. She was a running back, so she was shorter than Ronda and compact, like a little muscle machine. All Ronda knew about her was her last name was O'Reilly. And she had short dark hair. She was cute from a distance. Ronda was thinking about walking over to her when her friend Donna Spencer walked up.

"I see you checking out the new blood," Donna said. "You gonna say something to her?"

"I was getting ready to make my move when you walked up."

"Don't let me stand in your way."

"O'Reilly!" Coach Poehl, the head coach, said. "You're in."

"Well, hell," Ronda said. "There goes that opportunity."

"You'll be able to catch her in the locker room, I'm sure. And she might be just what you need after a long, hot shower."

"Meyers." Coach Hindley walked up. "Go soak in the tub. You played hard today."

"Yes, ma'am." Ronda didn't have to be asked twice to soak. Even though it was an ice bath, it still felt good after playing as hard as she had.

She soaked until her trainers told her her time was up. Then she joined the others in the locker room. She stripped and headed for the showers. Fortunately for her, O'Reilly was showering at the same time. Ronda knew it would be awkward to approach her while they were both naked, so she quickly showered and dried. She was dressed when she looked over and saw O'Reilly leaving. She quickened her step to catch up.

"O'Reilly, right?" Ronda said as they walked to their cars.

"Yep. Meyers, right?"

"Guilty."

O'Reilly laughed.

"I'd have to be an idiot not to know the league MVP."

Ronda stopped and put out her hand.

"I'm Ronda," she said.

"I'm Mallory."

"Mallory. It's nice to meet you."

"You, too."

"So, Mallory, can I take you to dinner tonight?" Ronda said.

"I've heard about you," Mallory said with a smile.

"So that's a no?"

"Actually, I think I'll take my chances. What time?"

"Seven?"

"Sounds good."

"Where can I pick you up?"

Mallory gave Ronda the address where she was staying and they said their good-byes. Ronda checked her watch. Damn. She had a half an hour before she was supposed to meet the Logans who were looking at the house. She stepped on it and arrived with twenty minutes to spare.

"You know I hate it when you don't get here a half hour early," Gayla said. "Come on. Let's go over everything."

Gayla handed her the flyer of information. Ronda looked over it and was ready when the Logans showed up five minutes early.

"And this is why you get here a half hour before the appointment," Gayla said.

"Relax, I'm ready. I'm going out to greet them. You just chill."

Ronda stepped out into the spring heat and waited as Oliver and Nadine Logan got out of the car.

"Hello again," Ronda said as she shook their hands. "I think we've found the perfect spot for you."

"I love it so far," Nadine said. "I love this yard."

"Well, it sits on a sixty-five hundred square foot lot," Ronda said. "And I know you love your gardening."

"I do."

Ronda guided them into the house itself.

"Now it's a two-bedroom, one-bath, just like you're looking for," she said.

"And the square footage?" Oliver said.

"It's fourteen hundred. So it's not too big for just the two of you."

She took them on a tour and showed them the bedrooms and the bath. It really was the perfect place for a young couple such as the Logans.

"I love it," Nadine said. "And it only took you three tries to find the perfect fit. You're wonderful, Ronda."

"Thanks. But it was all you two. You let me know exactly what you were looking for."

They discussed the asking price and then made an offer that Ronda thought was legitimate. She shook hands again with both of them before they got in their car and drove off.

Ronda walked into the kitchen where Gayle was sitting.

"So, this looks like a slam dunk," Ronda said.

"Great. Shall we go out and celebrate?"

Ronda checked her watch. It was five.

"Sure. Let's go grab a drink."

"You have plans?" Gayla said.

"Yeah, but not until seven, so we're good."

"Are you sure? I can take a rain check."

"No, come on. Let's go to Brownie's. I'll meet you there."

Gayla was somewhat somber.

"What gives?" Ronda said. "We're celebrating here. I just sold a seven-hundred-thousand-dollar house. And you look like you lost your best friend."

"I'm sorry. I am happy. Honest."

"Good. So let's drink."

Ronda ordered two margaritas and they found a seat in the bar area.

"So, what's happening at seven?" Gayla said.

"I'm taking a rookie to dinner."

"Oh? Who's the lucky lady?"

"Her name's Mallory O'Reilly. We just picked her up yesterday from New Orleans."

"And you're going to treat her to the ol' Meyers' hospitality, huh?"

"We'll see. Apparently, my reputation precedes me." She laughed.

"Oh, it does, huh? Well then, you may be sleeping alone after all."

"Maybe. But she agreed to dinner, so we'll just see what happens."

They finished their drinks and walked out to their cars.

"Good luck tonight," Gayla said.

"Thanks."

Ronda got back to her house and changed into something less formal for dinner. She chose gray slacks and a black golf shirt. She looked good and she knew it. She sprayed on a touch of her favorite cologne and called for a car.

She directed the car to the address Mallory had given her. It was a nice apartment complex not far from where she lived in River Oaks. She climbed the stairs and knocked on her door.

Mallory opened the door looking absolutely adorable in slacks and a green golf shirt. There would be no doubt they were lesbians wherever they went that night. Ronda smiled.

"So, I guess we're wearing our dyke uniforms tonight, huh?" she said.

"I guess so."

"You ready for some good Tex-Mex?"

"I guess I need to try it sometime. Now is as good a time as any."

Ronda gave the driver the address for the restaurant and settled in the back with Mallory.

"So, how are you feeling today after practice?"

"I didn't get many reps, so I'm not as worn out as you must be. Dang, they use you almost every down."

"Still, the calisthenics are a bitch."

"Yeah, but I've been doing them with New Orleans, so at least I'm in shape."

"You certainly are," Ronda said.

Mallory blushed.

"You don't even try to hide that you're a predator, do you?"

"Nope. And it's true. You're in great shape. That's from one player to another."

"Where on earth did you get the idea I'm a player?" Mallory said.

"No! Not that kind of player. Football player."

"Okay." Mallory laughed. "Okay. Fair enough."

The car pulled up in front of the restaurant. Ronda stepped out and let Mallory slide out before she closed the door.

"You're going to love it here," she said. "Do you like fajitas? They're known for fajitas."

"I have to admit I've never had good fajitas."

"Well, may I recommend that change tonight?"

"Sounds good to me."

They went inside and Ronda started moving to the groove of Tex-Mex music that was playing.

Mallory smiled but said nothing.

The hostess seated them outside, as it was a warm evening.

"Do I need to look at a menu?" Mallory said.

"Nope. We'll have margaritas to drink and steak fajitas to eat. Unless you're a vegetarian or something?"

"No worries there. I'm a meat eater."

"That's what I was hoping to hear." Ronda winked.

"You're plain evil." Mallory laughed. "Haven't you ever heard of playing coy?"

"Aw, come on. I'm just havin' some fun with you. It's all good."

"You are pretty funny. I'll give you that."

The waitress came by and Ronda ordered for both of them.

"So, how long have you been with the Stars?" Mallory asked.

"This is my seventh season."

"That's a whole career for most people."

"Yeah, well, I'm not most people."

"No, you're not," Mallory said.

Dinner was filled with quiet conversation about practices and all the new people Mallory was having to get to know and coordinate with out on the field.

"So, what's Canfield's story?" she asked.

Rebecca Canfield was their quarterback. And one of the best in the league.

"What do you mean?"

"I swear she was trying to make me look bad today. I'd think we'd all be working together, but she'd call a play for me to go right and she'd turn left, so I'd look like an idiot."

"Look," Ronda said. "Her girlfriend was our starting running back last year. She got traded last month. Maybe Canfield can't handle a replacement."

"Well, someone's gotta be her replacement, right? We need a running back. And we have barely a month before the season starts."

"I'll talk to her," Ronda said.

"No! You can't. I mean, I'd look like a total whiner."

"No. I won't ask about you. I'll just tell her she looks a little rusty and see if she wants to talk. I'll tell her to shake it off one way or another," Ronda said.

"Okay, but I won't be mentioned?"

"Not at all."

"Promise?"

"I swear," Ronda said.

"Good."

They finished their dinner and their drinks. Ronda had a full stomach and was in a mellow mood. She was also sitting with a hot little number, so her hormones were burning just under the surface.

"So," Ronda said. "I guess my next question is pretty obvious, huh?"

"If I'll want to see you again?"

It was like a blow to the gut. She could almost feel her ego deflating. She recovered quickly.

"Yes. I'd like to see you again."

"That wasn't what you were asking and you know it." Mallory laughed. "Come on. Let's get out of here."

Ronda stood and followed Mallory out of the restaurant. Or tried to. She was stopped three times and asked for her autograph. She tried to be gracious, but just wanted to tell the guys asking that she was just about to get laid. She knew better and had a good chuckle over the thought.

"What's so funny?" Mallory asked when Ronda finally made it out.

"Nothing. Nothing at all."

They sat together in the back of the car.

"You know, we have practice at ten tomorrow."

"Don't worry. I won't keep you up too late."

"You don't know that," Mallory said. "I may be one of those women who takes forever."

"Are you?"

"No."

"Good."

They got out of the car and headed for the house.

"Which would you prefer first? The bed or the Jacuzzi tub?" Ronda asked.

"Oh, a tub sounds wonderful," Mallory said.

Ronda led her back to the master bathroom. She turned the tub on and set the bubbles churning. Then she turned to Mallory. She pulled her shirt off and then removed her bra.

"Your uniform doesn't do you justice," Ronda said. "You're all woman under those pads."

"Yes, I am."

Ronda held one breast in both hands. She bent and took Mallory's nipple in her mouth. She sucked it hard. It responded by growing in her mouth and pressing against the roof of her mouth.

"Damn, woman," Ronda said, but Mallory didn't respond. She was holding on to Ronda's shoulders, her eyes shut tight. "You've got some fine titties on you."

Ronda unbuttoned Mallory's slacks. She unzipped them and they dropped to the floor.

"You want to get those shoes off so I can see you naked?" Ronda said.

Mallory kicked off her shoes and stepped out of her pants.

"Oh, yeah," Ronda said. "That's what I call a body."

Mallory was much curvier than Gayla, but her curves were right where they needed to be.

"Your turn," Mallory said. "Let me get a look at what all the fuss is about."

Ronda laughed.

"The fuss?"

"Sure. The body that's worth however much they insure you for."

"Oh, please. As far as I know, that's just a rumor." Ronda took her shirt off.

"I'm sure it's not."

Ronda finished stripping and turned off the water. She stood naked for Mallory's inspection.

"Shit, woman, there's not an ounce of fat on you," Mallory said.

Ronda closed the distance between them and lifted Mallory's chin. She gazed into her blue eyes, dark with passion. She lowered her mouth and tasted Mallory's. Her lips were soft and tender. And Ronda needed more.

"Let's get in the water," she said. They sat next to each other and Ronda placed her arm around Mallory and pulled her close. She closed her mouth on Mallory's again. This time she ran her tongue along her lower lip until Mallory opened her mouth for her. Ronda slid her tongue inside and found her warm and moist. Her desire soared as their tongues met and danced together. She never wanted the kiss to end, but eventually, Mallory broke it.

"Damn, you sure know how to kiss," Mallory said.

"I'd say we do pretty good together."

She ran her hand along the water until it was under one of Mallory's breasts. She bent to take her nipple in her mouth again. She sucked hard and ran her tongue all over it.

"Oh, shit, Ronda."

It was so much fun playing with her breast. She wanted to spend the whole night right there, but knew there was more to explore. She dropped the breast and ran her hand down her body to between her legs. She found her clit swollen and her lips wet.

"Oh, yeah, you're ready for me, aren't you?" Ronda said.

She kissed her again. A deep, passionate kiss that made her toes curl. Ronda slid her fingers inside Mallory, as deep as they would go. She pulled them out, then thrust them back in. She made sure to keep the palm of her hand on Mallory's clit as she plunged her fingers in and out until Mallory grabbed her wrist and held it still.

"Jesus, oh Jesus," Mallory said. "Oh, Jesus, yes. Oh, God, yes. Oh, yes."

Ronda kept her hand where it was until Mallory relaxed back against the wall of the tub.

"So I guess we got there?" she said.

"Hell yes."

Ronda smiled a big smile.

"Right on." Then she said, "Let's hit the bed."

They got out and toweled off. Ronda led the way to the bed. She lay down and pulled Mallory on top of her.

"Easy, there, Ronda. I weigh more than I look like I do."

"I'm not worried."

"Well, I am. I don't want to have to explain a boudoir injury to Coach Hindley." She laughed.

"Fair enough. But you didn't hurt me."

Mallory rolled off Ronda and lay there running her hand up and down her body.

"I love your body," she said.

"Like you admire it or you want it?"

"A little of both, I suppose. It's natural to admire it, but damn, I want it, too."

"Then take me, Mal. Fuck me senseless."

Mallory sucked one of Ronda's nipples into her mouth and took half her breast with it. She teased the other with her fingers while she sucked the one.

"Oh, yeah. Now we're talkin'," Ronda said.

Mallory let loose of the nipple and kissed down Ronda's belly until she was between her legs. She pried her legs wide and got comfortable. She licked and nipped at Ronda's hard clit before lapping at the juices flowing inside her.

Ronda had her hand on Mallory's head, tangling in her dark hair. Mallory moved back to Ronda's clit and sucked it between her lips. She flicked the tip of it with her tongue until Ronda cried out as she came.

CHAPTER THREE

The next day, as the team left the locker room for the field, Ronda made her way to Canfield.

"You doin' okay, Canfield?" she said.

"Yeah. Why?"

"You look a little rusty out there. I'd hate to see you lose your starting position just because you miss your girl."

"I don't know what you're talking about."

"I'm just sayin' your girl isn't coming back. One of these running backs has to be a starter. And you're not making them look bad out there. You're making it look like you don't know the playbook. So get it together, huh?"

"Fuck you, Meyers. You focus on defense and let me focus on offense."

"Suit yourself, but if you need to talk, I'm here."

Ronda was on the sideline again when O'Reilly was called to go in. Ronda watched and Canfield looked much more coordinated. Ronda smiled to herself. She was glad Mallory wouldn't look like a fool on the field.

❖

Saturday evening arrived. It was a time Ronda had been dreading. Gayla had booked her for another fundraiser. This one was to benefit a local children's program. Ronda was all about helping raise money for the kids, but she was exhausted and didn't feel like pressing the flesh.

She dressed in a black suit with a white shirt, which she knew would be appropriate. She'd already checked with Gayla. Gayla was as excited as she could be. Ronda was barely able to relax with a drink due to all the texts Gayla was sending.

Gayla showed up at Ronda's house early. She looked dynamite in her blue cocktail dress. It was a tight number, with a strap over her right shoulder. It showed off her cleavage in the most delightful way.

"You look great, babe." Ronda kissed her cheek.

"Thanks. So do you."

"Should I put on a blue shirt? You know, so we match?"

"No. You look fine just how you are."

"You know, you're crimping my style, booking all my Saturday nights with events. I need to be able to go out and let loose sometimes."

"I'm sorry, loverboi, but the closer we get to the season, the more events we have."

"Ugh." She sat in her favorite recliner. She seemed to have forgotten Gayla was there as she took another sip of scotch. "I'm sorry. I should have offered you a drink."

"I know where to find the booze." Gayla crossed the room to the bar. She came back to stand in front of Ronda.

"Do I have any showings tomorrow?" Ronda said.

"Nope. Remember? You asked me to clear the day for you."

"I don't remember that at all. Thank God you're my brains."

Gayla sat on the couch across from Ronda and crossed her legs.

"Baby, I'll be whatever you need me to be."

"You just keep being my brains and my part-time bedmate and I'll be happy. Which, by the way, I'm hoping you'll want to be tonight. Because, babe, you're on fire."

"I love that you think so. If you do, so might everybody else."

Ronda wondered anew if Gayla truly dressed for the crowds or if she was the one she tried to impress. It didn't matter. The crowds would appreciate her as Ronda's date for the night.

"So, what's the deal tonight? How long do we have to stay?"
Gayla laughed.

"You're funny. We're not even there yet and you're trying to leave. Relax. You just might have fun."

"I might. But I doubt it." She set her drink down and called for the car. "We've got about ten minutes."

"Just enough time to mess up my makeup," Gayla said.

"Huh?"

"Never mind."

"Oh. I get it. Very funny." She looked hard at Gayla.

"What?" Gayla said.

"Nothing. Sometimes I wonder."

"What?"

"How serious you are about me?"

"Serious? Please. You're not the only one who goes out and lets loose."

"Okay. I'm sorry. I guess it's just my ego."

"No, dear. Okay, well, maybe partially. But it's also your unnatural fear of commitment. I'm surprised you invited me to stay tonight. That's two Saturdays in a row. Anyone else might start getting ideas."

"I know you won't. I might momentarily freak, but I know, deep down, you know better."

"I think the car's here." Gayla walked to the window.

Ronda crossed the room to stand behind her. She ground herself into her ass. It felt good. She reached around and pulled Gayla back into her.

"You sure you don't want to skip this thing?" Ronda said.

"We look too good to waste it."

They climbed in the car and were whooshed off to the Children's Museum. As Ronda stepped out, the flashes began and didn't stop until she and Gayla had made their way inside.

"How many photographers were out there?" Ronda whispered in Gayla's ear.

"Not that many, I don't think. I think a lot of regular people were out there, too."

A woman who looked to be in her fifties approached them.

"Ronda Meyers? This is such a pleasure. I'm Carleen Brynes. I'm the chair tonight." She extended her hand and Ronda took it. It was soft and Ronda fought the urge to press her lips to it. Her face was kind and her short-cropped silver hair really showed off her blue eyes. She was gorgeous. Ronda felt the familiar twinge deep inside. It took her a moment to recover.

"This is Gayla Adkins," she said as she stepped aside. "Gayla, Carleen."

"It's wonderful to meet you," Gayla said. "And Ronda has been so excited for this event. She loves children."

Ronda listened and made herself not shake her head. Something happened to Gayla at these events. She just transformed into someone else. Ronda wished she could do the same thing. She supposed she must to some extent. Otherwise, no one would invite her to them.

"Well, let's get you two some champagne," Carleen said. She linked her hand through Ronda's elbow. "Lead on, mighty one."

Ronda laughed, a genuine laugh. Gayla arched an eyebrow at her as she walked along on the other side.

"So, Carleen," Ronda said when they reached the table of champagne. "How did you end up working with this organization?"

"I love children and I love books. It was only natural that I set up a foundation to get children more involved in reading."

"That's awesome."

"Are you a big reader?" Carleen said.

"Ronda really doesn't have time to read much with her busy schedule," Gayla said.

Carleen looked over as if she'd forgotten Gayla was there.

"I do read the sport section of the paper," Ronda said. "To follow our competitors, you know?"

"Of course." Carleen laughed and placed her hand on Ronda's forearm.

Ronda really liked Carleen and wanted to get her away from the crowds. She wanted to see if this lover of children was also a lover of women. But that didn't seem likely to happen as the crowd pressed in on them.

"I think we need to mingle," Gayla said. "I'll head that way and you two head this way?"

"I think that sounds wonderful," Carleen said. "Come on, Ronda. Let's press the flesh."

"I do love pressing flesh," Ronda said. Gayla shot her a look. What was it? Jealousy? Ronda didn't know. She smiled at her and allowed herself to be guided by Carleen.

As they moved through the crowd, they stopped to sign autographs on balls, posters, and books. Someone asked Ronda how she felt about the foundation.

"I think it's great. Kids reading means fewer kids on the street," Ronda said. She received a warm round of applause. She caught Gayla watching her. She arched an eyebrow and was treated to a smile and a nod.

"Are you getting warm?" Carleen said. "We could step outside for some air."

"I don't know that it won't be just as warm out there, but at least the air will be fresh," Ronda said.

They stepped out onto the back patio.

"Oh, this is nice," Ronda said.

"It really is. You're doing wonderfully in there. You're a natural. You must really enjoy these events."

"I do okay," Ronda said. "Sometimes they're hard. But thank you. You're making this one easy."

"It's my pleasure. To escort one of Houston's most eligible bachelorettes for an evening is no skin off my nose."

Ronda laughed a deep belly laugh.

"That's funny."

"You are, you know. There are a lot of women who would kill to be me tonight."

"I don't think so. But thank you. You're certainly good for my ego."

Carleen stood in front of Ronda and looked deep into her eyes.

"I'm quite sure of it. I'd be a fool not to recognize that."

Ronda stood still, unsure what was expected of her. Should she kiss Carleen? She wanted to, but was Carleen just playing the happy hostess? Ronda was saved when Gayla walked out onto the patio to join them.

"People are asking where you've gone," she said. "My whole side of the room is geared up and ready to meet you."

"I just needed a little fresh air," Ronda said. "We can get back to it now."

"Great. Come on." Gayla linked her hand through one elbow while Carleen did the same with the other. They went to the opposite side of the room and the people there erupted with cheers when they saw Ronda.

"Ronda Meyers!" someone yelled.

"You're the greatest!" someone else called.

It was all very heady for Ronda, who knew she was the best on the football field, but hearing it from fans struck a note in her.

"Thank you," she said and smiled at her followers.

She proceeded through the crowd and shook hands with the fifty or so fans who were there.

"Have you made your donation?" she asked every time she stopped to sign something.

The night progressed smoothly and people were finally starting to make their way out of the place.

"How are you doing?" Gayla whispered.

"Get me out of here," Ronda whispered back.

"Oh, Ronda," Carleen said. "Tonight has been such a success. Thank you so much for this. And if I can do anything for you, anything at all, don't you dare hesitate to ask."

Ronda felt her slip something in her jacket pocket but knew better than to take it out and look at it with Gayla there. She hoped it was a phone number. She'd love to spend more time with Carleen.

Ronda shook her hand.

"It's been a pleasure. Thank you for the wonderful work you do."

"And thank you," Carleen said to Gayla. "I appreciate all your help tonight."

"My pleasure. Now it's time for me to get Ronda home before she turns into a pumpkin."

"Fair enough." Carleen laughed. Her blue eyes sparkled. "I'll see you both around."

They climbed into the car and Ronda let out a long sigh, happy the event was over, even though time with Carleen had been enjoyable.

"So what did I interrupt out there?" Gayla said.

"Huh?"

"On the patio. Something was going on. Had you just kissed her?"

"What? No. We were talking. That's all."

"She had a guilty look on her face."

"Well, maybe she had something goin' on in her mind, but I didn't touch her. And who cares if I did?"

"It's not a big deal. I was just wondering."

"Well, no. Nothing happened."

They drove to Ronda's house and Ronda held Gayla's hand as she climbed out of the car. She pulled her against her.

"You're the only one I've been thinking about kissing tonight," she said.

"I so don't believe you, but it's okay. I don't own you."

"No, but I had promised to be with you tonight, so I don't want you to think I was hitting on someone else or thinking about leaving you high and dry."

"I wouldn't have been dry, baby."

"No." She smiled. "I don't suppose you would have been."

Ronda kissed Gayla softly on her lips.

"I love kissing you," she said.

"Then do it again," Gayla said.

Ronda kissed her again, harder. She let her tongue wander into Gayla's mouth and felt the familiar stirring that came from kissing her. She released her and led her up the stairs and inside.

"Would you like something to drink?"

"Sure. I'd love a scotch."

Ronda poured two of them and walked over to the sofa where Gayla sat. She sat next to her.

"Babe, you rocked that place tonight," Ronda said. "You outshone everyone there."

"I think that would be you," Gayla said. "You were the most handsome person there, male or female."

"Thank you," Ronda said. "I felt in my groove tonight. I didn't feel all robotic and on display. I don't know what was different."

"I think it was Carleen. I think you like her."

"She was a very attractive woman."

"You should have invited her home to play with us."

Ronda stopped, glass halfway to her lips.

"What did you just say?"

Gayla laughed.

"What? You've never done that before? I have a hard time believing that. You may be younger than I am, but I doubt you're any more innocent."

"Wow," Ronda said. "Just wow. I can't believe we're having this talk. Actually, we're not. I refuse to have this talk with you."

"Fine. But I still kind of wish you'd invited Carleen home with us."

"I want to spend this night focused on you. Only you. You took my breath away the minute you walked in wearing that dress. I wanted to peel it off you as soon as I saw you. It didn't cross my mind to add another variable to our equation."

"Fair enough." She snuggled closer to Ronda. "I just want you to know, if the opportunity comes up, I'm open to it."

Ronda felt odd. For a moment, she was jealous. Yes, jealous and she was a big enough woman to admit it. To herself, not to anyone else. But next came the arousal. Watching Gayla and Carleen make love would have been totally hot.

"Whatcha thinkin' handsome?" Gayla said.

"Just kind of considering that. Wondering what it would be like to have a threesome with you."

Gayla hiked her dress up around her waist and straddled Ronda's lap.

"It would be just like the two of us but with one more person to please and be pleased by."

Ronda ran her hands up Gayla's thighs until she could feel the heat radiating from within.

"But it takes so much concentration to please you. I'd hate to miss a suck or a stroke because someone was distracting me."

"Ronda Meyers. Are you telling me you've never had a three-way?"

"I'm just saying I can't imagine a three-way with you. I don't like to share."

"You're so sweet. Careful. A girl could get ideas."

"No, you won't."

She pulled Gayla to her and kissed her again, the taste of scotch sweet on her mouth.

Gayla unbuckled Ronda's belt. Next she unbuttoned her slacks and unzipped them. She slid her hand inside and found Ronda drenched. Ronda ground her teeth together to keep from crying out at Gayla's knowing touch.

"Relax, baby," Gayla cooed into Ronda's ear. "Let it happen."

Ronda tried to stand, but found her legs unsteady. Gayla helped her up then knelt before her to take off her shoes. She helped Ronda step out of her slacks and boxers. Ronda liked looking down to see Gayla looking up at her, knowing what she was looking at.

Gayla kissed up Ronda's inner thighs.

"No," Ronda said. "I can't hold my balance."

She sat down and Gayla spread her legs and licked the length of her. She lapped at her juices and sucked her clit. She flicked her tongue over it and Ronda climaxed almost immediately.

"Damn, woman. What happened to ladies first?"

"Not tonight. You looked too good. I had to have you and have you as soon as I could. I didn't want to wait. I wanted you before the gig, you may remember."

"I do remember." Ronda sat there trying to catch her breath. "That was intense. And it happened so quickly. You're gonna start rumors I'm easy."

"I'll never breathe a word of it to anyone," Gayla said. "Now get me out of this dress."

Ronda stood and rubbed her hand over Gayla's exposed shoulder.

"Your skin is so smooth," she said. She bent to kiss her shoulder and got to inhale Gayla's light fragrance. "And you smell so good."

"You're making me crazy," Gayla said.

"Just because you got me off so fast doesn't mean I won't take my time with you."

"Honey, I can't help but take you fast. I take one look at you and I melt."

"Well, let me return the favor. Let's go back to my room where we can get comfortable."

When they got to Ronda's bedroom, she unzipped Gayla's dress.

"I always feel so bad when I take the wrapping off my presents," Ronda said.

"Huh?"

"You always look so damned good in those dresses. Don't get me wrong, I love you naked, but it's a sad thing to have to take the dresses off to get to the goods."

"I think I know what you're saying so I won't take offense."

"Good. Please don't. I'm a football player. Not a poet."

Gayla laughed.

"This is true."

Ronda kissed Gayla on the mouth then as she unhooked her bra and tossed it on top of her dress. She kissed down her body until she got to her panties, which she pulled down and helped Gayla step out of.

She eased her back onto the bed and sucked one nipple and then the other.

"Damn, you've got the best tits," Ronda said.

"I do believe you've mentioned that."

"I just love holding them and sucking them."

"Well, you sure know how to make them feel good, so please keep doing what you're doing."

Ronda continued to suck on her nipple as she ran her hand down her body to where her legs met. She teased Gayla's clit briefly before entering her. She moved her fingers in and out until Gayla was bucking on the bed, keeping time with her.

Finally, Ronda moved her fingers back to Gayla's clit and rubbed it until Gayla tangled her fingers in Ronda's hair and called out her name.

"There you go, baby," Ronda said. "Now you just relax."

"How could I do anything else?"

Chapter Four

With nothing on her agenda the next day, Ronda lay in bed an extra long time. She spent part of it dozing and part of it watching Gayla sleep. When she could finally stand it no longer, she got out of bed and went to the kitchen to make coffee. She stretched, her back sore from the extra time in bed.

The coffee was brewing and Ronda flashed back to Carleen from the night before. What had she slipped in her pocket? She went into the bedroom and took a business card from her jacket pocket. On the back was a cell number. Ronda smiled. She would definitely give her a call. Why not? She was a beautiful woman.

She went back to the kitchen and used a magnet to stick the card to her refrigerator. She was just about to pour a cup of coffee when Gayla walked in.

"Whatcha doin' hot stuff?" she said.

"Just getting some caffeine. Can I get you some?"

"Sure."

Gayla perused Ronda's refrigerator while Ronda poured the coffee.

"Well, lookie here," Gayla said. "Someone scored a business card from Carleen."

"Yeah, I did. Pretty cool, huh?"

"Very cool. Are you going to call her?"

"I thought I might." Ronda was silent for a second. "You know it's kinda weird to be having this conversation while we're standing here naked."

"Baby, you know I don't care who you sleep with."

"I know, but it's still strange."

"Well, I'm not going to put my clothes on until you make me. I was kind of hoping us both being naked might lead to more sex."

"You were, huh?" Ronda took Gayla in her arms. She loved the contrast of her dark skin with Gayla's white skin. She lifted her up and set her on the kitchen counter.

"Ronda! You're going to hurt yourself if you keep doing stuff like that."

"I know my strength," Ronda said. "Don't you worry about me."

"You'd better. You strain anything and I need to explain it, well, we'll both be in trouble."

"Don't you worry."

Ronda sucked a nipple deep into her mouth. She ran her tongue over it.

Gayla groaned. She clamped her hands over Ronda's head and held her in place.

"Yes. Oh, yes, baby."

Ronda was hot and getting hotter by the moment. She wanted to take Gayla to places she'd never been before.

"Don't move," she said.

"What the…Where are you going?"

"Just stay there," Ronda called over her shoulder as she walked down the hall.

She came back and Gayla was sitting up, legs together.

"Hey, what gives?" Ronda asked.

"You left. I didn't feel like sitting here like a jezebel."

"Oh, babe. You're not a jezebel. You're a beautiful woman I want to please with every ounce of me."

"So, why did you leave then?

Ronda brought her arm from behind her back. In her hand was a long, thick dildo.

"I want to fill you up, Gayla. I want to make you feel things you've never felt."

Gayla's eyes grew wide.

"I don't know if I can take all that, Ronda."

"Well, I say we try. Now, relax and spread those legs again."

Ronda set the dildo down and spread Gayla's legs so she could stand between them. She then went back to playing with Gayla's nipples. She sucked one while she tugged and twisted the other.

She moved her hand to Gayla's pussy and found her very wet. She slipped a couple of fingers inside. She spread them out then pulled them back out. She did this several times. She took her fingers out and sucked them clean.

"Damn, you taste good."

"Oh, my God, Ronda, what are you doing?"

"I'm tasting you."

Ronda picked up the dildo. She ran it along the length of Gayla.

"I'm scared," Gayla said.

"Don't be. Relax."

She barely entered Gayla with just the tip.

"How does that feel?"

"More. I need more."

Ronda smiled.

"I thought you'd say that."

She eased a little more in. The toy was halfway inside Gayla.

"Just fuck me with it, baby. I can take it," Gayla said.

Ronda slid the dildo the rest of the way in. She pushed hard on it then slid it back out. Then, slowly she entered her again.

"Oh, God, Ronda. Stop teasing me. Fuck me hard and fast. That feels so fucking good."

Ronda was happy to oblige. She sucked a nipple while she fucked Gayla with the toy. In and out and in and out she went. Gayla arched her hips and met every thrust.

Finally, she pulled Ronda to her and cried out as the orgasms racked her body.

"Wow," she said. "That was awesome."

"Yeah? Good. I'm glad you enjoyed it. I'm going to take it out now, okay?"

"Hm? Yeah. Okay."

Her body held tight to it, but eventually Ronda managed to ease it out. She went to the kitchen sink and washed it off.

"So." She turned back to Gayla. "I guess it was worth it to stay naked, huh?"

"Hell yeah, baby." She laughed.

Ronda helped Gayla down from the kitchen counter and poured them each a cup of coffee. Gayla took hers black, but Ronda added a generous amount of chocolate milk to hers.

"I want to go for a swim," Gayla said.

"Sounds good to me."

Gayla opened the slider and Ronda followed her out to the patio and the pool beyond. Ronda's backyard was full of live oak trees, pecan trees, and banana trees. There was no way her neighbors could see them.

They dove in the pool and swam around until they came together in the shallow end.

"I love to watch your muscles ripple as you swim," Gayla said.

"Hush, woman. You're going to make me blush."

"The great Ronda Meyers does not blush. Believe me. I'd know if you did."

Ronda swam to the other end of the pool and pulled herself out. She sat on the diving board and watched Gayla.

"You sure don't sit very ladylike," Gayla said.

"Nope. I never have. So what?"

"So, you're like an open invitation there."

"Come and get it."

Gayla swam over to that end of the pool.

"I don't think I can get you from this angle."

"Well, then, we'll just have to wait."

"I don't want to wait. Turn around and lie on your back."

Ronda did as she was instructed. She straddled the board with her legs.

"Perfect," Gayla said as she climbed out of the pool.

With no pretense, Gayla bent down and licked Ronda. She sucked her wet lips and licked her swollen clit. Ronda closed her eyes and focused on the feelings. Gayla made her feel so good. She knew her body like no one else. Ronda felt the familiar tightening in her belly. She focused on it, willing herself to hold on a little longer, but she could not. The energy inside her burst forth as the waves of the orgasms crashed over her.

"Damn, woman." Ronda sat up.

"I know, right?"

"Right."

"I suppose I should get going, huh?" Gayla said.

"What's that? A wham-bam-thank-you-ma'am?"

"No. Not at all. I just don't want to overstay my welcome."

"Ah. I do appreciate that, but you're not. You're good. Trust me. You want to take a nap?"

"No. I really do think I need to get home."

"No nap? I was thinking nap then sex."

"That is so tempting."

Gayla had no idea how tempting it was, Ronda thought. She could spend the whole day playing with her.

"But I need to get going."

"Fine. I'll walk you inside."

Ronda draped her arm across Gayla's shoulders and they walked in the house together. Ronda lay naked on the bed as she watched Gayla get dressed in her finery from the previous evening.

"This isn't fair," Gayla said. "Couldn't you at least put something on?"

"Why? If I'm just going to take a nap."

"Damn, you're incorrigible."

"Thank you."

Ronda got up and pulled on some shorts.

"Better?"

"Yes." Gayla tossed her a T-shirt.

Ronda put it on as well.

"I feel awfully overdressed for my own house on a day when I have nothing to do."

"You're going to walk me to my car. And that's outside. And unless you want all your neighbors to get a free show, you need clothes on. Now quit whining and walk me out."

Ronda laughed. Gayla was so funny. And so easy to be around. She was kind of bummed she wasn't going to spend the day with her. But she got it. Gayla had a life. She had things to do. And as rare as it was for Ronda to have a day off, it was a rarer day for Gayla.

"You'll text me with a schedule for next week?"

"Don't you worry, handsome. Momma's not going to leave you in the wind. You'll know your schedule as soon as I do."

"Thanks." She kissed her cheek and watched her drive off.

Ronda stretched and walked back in the house. A whole day off. No practice, no houses to show, no fundraiser. She wondered what she should do with her day. She sat on her couch and flipped on the television. There was nothing good on. She went to the kitchen to get another cup of coffee. Carleen's card from the night before caught her attention.

She could give her a call. No, too soon. She wanted to spend some time with her, though. She was gorgeous and made Ronda's blood run hot. And maybe Gayla was right. Maybe she was about to kiss Ronda the previous night. Still, it was too soon. Or maybe not. She wasn't sure. She needed more caffeine and food and then she would figure out what to do.

When she was properly fed and caffeinated, Ronda drove to the Stars' practice facilities. She found Mack, the maintenance man, and got into the film room. Someone was already in there.

She turned to Mack and thanked him, then walked up to see who was there.

"Oh, hey Mallory."

"Hi. What's up? I didn't think anyone else would be here."

"I got bored."

"Me, too."

"Well, since you're already here, I'll head out. Enjoy the film." Mallory stood.

"No, I've seen enough."

Ronda put her hand on Mallory's shoulder.

"No offense, Mallory, but you've got a lot more to learn than I do."

"That's true. Would it help if I told you I've already been here two hours?"

"No shit? Okay. You've seen enough. Hey, you want to go do something together? You golf?"

"I try."

"Let's get some beers and give it a shot."

"Sounds good to me."

Mallory followed Ronda to the Country Club golf course. Ronda kept an eye on her rearview mirror to make sure she didn't lose her. She liked the sparkplug and was hoping an afternoon of golf might lead to more.

They picked up a six-pack of beer and hit the links. Mallory was surprisingly good. Ronda was glad they hadn't wagered, because Mallory didn't just try. She knew what she was doing out there. By the ninth hole, it was getting embarrassing.

"You're spankin' my ass," Ronda said.

"I love golf," Mallory said. "I just didn't know I was any good at it."

"Well, clearly you are."

They finished the course with Mallory nine strokes under Ronda. They went to the clubhouse for beers.

"Damn. I'm glad we didn't bet."

"What would you have bet me?" Mallory said.

"I don't know…"

"Who comes first?"

Ronda looked around the room, but Mallory had said it quietly enough.

"Don't worry," Mallory said. "No one heard."

"That's my kind of bet. And you won."

"But we didn't actually bet."

"I'm willing to pretend we did."

Before Mallory could say anything, a voice came from behind Ronda.

"Ronda? Ronda Meyers?"

The voice was familiar, but Ronda braced herself for a fan. She turned and found herself looking into the deep blue eyes of Carleen.

She stood and kissed her on the cheek.

"Carleen. How good to see you."

"It's good to see you, too, Ronda. I didn't realize you golfed."

"I try. Oh, where are my manners. This is Mallory O'Reilly. She's a new running back for the Stars. Hopefully, you'll be seeing a lot of her this year. Mallory, this is Carleen Brynes."

Mallory stood and shook Carleen's hand.

"I was thinking about calling you to see if you wanted to go out sometime," Ronda heard herself say.

"That would be lovely. Please do. I'll leave you two alone now."

She turned and walked off and Ronda watched her go.

"She's a looker," Mallory said.

"Yeah, she is."

"And you're going to take her out? Of course you are."

"Hey. She gave me her number. What am I supposed to do? Ignore her?"

"Hell no. If I had an invitation to that…" She shook her head slowly. "Mm. Yeah."

"I know, right?"

They sat back down and Ronda ordered another couple of beers.

"Now, about our wager."

"Our *imaginary* wager."

Ronda laughed.

"Whatever. I'd be happy to have you come over and hang out with me this evening. We can get some food and then go back to my place."

"You know, people say you're a player, but they don't say you're such a sweetheart. Or that you're drop-dead gorgeous."

"Whoa there, sister. I'm just me."

"No way. Your pictures do not do you justice, Ronda."

"Well, my photos in the programs aren't supposed to be like head shots. They're supposed to make me look like a badass who's going to rip your head off."

"That they do."

"Good. So, shall we get out of here?"

"Sure."

Ronda took Mallory to a family owned steakhouse for dinner that night. The food was great and the atmosphere lively. When a band started playing, Ronda stood and motioned Mallory to join her.

Mallory shook her head and looked at her hands in her lap.

Ronda sat down.

"What's up?" she said.

"I'm not as out as you are, I guess. And this is Houston. You know, Texas. I can't imagine they like to see two women dancing together."

"Fair enough. Next time we'll go to a lesbian joint where no one will care, okay?"

"Next time?" Mallory looked at Ronda.

"Sure. Why the hell not?"

They finished dinner and Mallory followed Ronda to her house. It was still fairly early, but that worked for both of them. They could take their time and enjoy each other's bodies and still get to bed in time to get up for early practice the next day.

"I feel like a swim. How self-conscious would you be if we swam in the nude?"

"I'd be fine," Mallory said. "It's not like you haven't seen my body before. Or that you won't see it again."

"True."

Ronda took Mallory's shirt off over her head. She looked so cute in her shorts and sports bra. She was so middle of the road. Not too butch. Not too femme. Just right. And she was adorable.

"What?" Mallory said.

"Nothing. Just admiring the view."

Mallory took her bra off.

"How about admiring this view?"

"Oh, I do like this," Ronda said. She cupped Mallory's breasts gently in her hands. She ran her thumbs over her nipples. "I like this very much."

Mallory snaked her arms behind Ronda's neck and pulled her down so their lips met. Ronda opened her mouth and let Mallory's tongue wander inside. She was not used to being the non-aggressor, but if it worked for Mallory, then she'd go with it. For a while.

Mallory finally broke the kiss.

"That was somethin' else," Ronda said.

"Yeah, it was."

"You're quite a little kisser."

"So are you. Though you're not so little."

"No, I've got a few inches on you."

"Just a few."

They laughed. Then Ronda unzipped Mallory's shorts and slid them off. Next came her boxers, and soon Mallory stood there in all her glory for Ronda to admire.

"You are one fine specimen," Ronda said.

"No fair. I want to see you naked, too. I love your body."

Ronda stripped so they were both naked, standing in the kitchen. Ronda stepped forward to feel their skin pressed together. The moisture pooled between her legs. She bent to kiss Mallory, and this time it was she who begged entrance into Mallory's mouth. Mallory parted her lips and Ronda moved her tongue inside and grew more aroused as it danced over Mallory's.

When the kiss ended, they were both breathing hard. Ronda wanted Mallory. She reached her hand between Mallory's legs. She was drenched.

"I need you," Ronda said.

"I thought you said something about skinny dipping," Mallory said.

How could she even be thinking about that at a time like this?

"Sex first," Ronda said.

She led Mallory back to her bedroom and froze when she saw Gayla's panties on the floor. How had that happened? She kicked them under the bed, but not before Mallory saw them.

"I don't think I'm you're only one. Don't worry about it. Now, take me."

They lay together on the bed with Mallory on top of Ronda. Ronda bent her knee so Mallory could slide up and down her thigh. Ronda played with first one breast and sucked one nipple, then the other. She was a breast woman and loved the ones that Mallory had.

Mallory moved up and down on Ronda's leg. She left a wet trail that had Ronda about to explode without being touched. She rolled over and ran her hand between Mallory's legs. She plunged her fingers inside and was rewarded when Mallory arched to take them deeper. Soon she was coated in her juices and getting hotter by the moment.

Ronda took her fingers out and rubbed Mallory's clit until Mallory grabbed her wrist.

"Oh, yeah. That's it. Oh, God. Oh, yes. Oh, Ronda. Oh, *yes*."

Ronda buried her face in Mallory's neck to hide her smile. She was so damned cute when she came.

Mallory wasted no time assuming her position between Ronda's legs. She lazily dragged her tongue over every inch of her.

"You taste so damned good," she said.

Ronda placed her hand on the back of Mallory's head to encourage her. Mallory licked inside her before moving her tongue to Ronda's swollen clit. She licked and flicked it and soon Ronda could hold out no longer. She closed her eyes tight. The bright colors began to shoot behind her eyelids just as she reached her powerful orgasm.

"You sure know how to use your tongue," Ronda said.

"Yeah?" Mallory looked cocky. "Just because I'm young doesn't mean I'm inexperienced."

Ronda laughed.

"Yeah? So I'm not the biggest player in the league?"

"Oh," Mallory said. "I think you are. Hands down."

"I can own that."

"Now, about that swim?" Mallory said.

CHAPTER FIVE

The swim? Ronda barely had the energy to lie there, much less get up and get in the pool.

"Ah, yes. I do believe I promised you skinny-dipping, didn't I?"

"Yes, you did. And as hot as you got me, I'm thinking that's just what I'll need to cool down. At least a little."

"Fair enough."

They walked out to the pool. Ronda draped her arm around Mallory's shoulders. They were much lower than Gayla's.

Gayla? What the hell was she doing in Ronda's mind when Ronda had another lover over?

She shook it off and dove into the pool.

"Are you coming?" she asked when she surfaced.

"I just did."

"Ha. You're a funny girl."

"I like to think so. I'm also not the kind to dive right in. I like to ease into it."

"That's not how you played it with me." Ronda swam to the edge of the pool.

"You're different," Mallory said.

"How so?"

"I can't explain it. I guess because I knew of you. I knew your reputation. I didn't have to worry about having an escape plan ready. I knew I wouldn't need one with you."

"I guess I see that."

Mallory walked down to the steps at the shallow end of the pool. She took one step in, then two. The water teased her just where her legs met. The light shown on her, and Ronda was wet with need again.

"How's that water feel?" she said.

"Feels good."

"Yeah? I bet. I wouldn't mind being that water right now."

"Come on over."

Ronda swam over and knelt on one of the stairs. She eased Mallory down on the top step.

"What do you think you're doing?" Mallory said.

"What do you think?"

She spread Mallory's legs and placed them over her shoulders. She moved her tongue all over. She licked and sucked and lapped and flicked. Then she slipped her fingers inside and waited to hear the usual from her.

"Oh, God. Oh, Jesus. Sweet Jesus. Oh, Ronda. Oh, Ronda."

This time Ronda had nowhere to hide her smile. She just beamed at how cute Mallory was.

"What?" Mallory said.

"What what?"

"You're all smiles. Are you proud of yourself?"

"No." Ronda laughed. "It's just that you're so fucking cute when you come."

"What's that mean?"

"Just what I said."

"I don't get it. Damn it. Now I'm going to be all self-conscious when I come. With whoever I come with. Damn you, Meyers."

"Meyers, huh? What happened to Ronda?"

"I'm mad at you."

"No, you're not. You have a thing when you come. It's cute. Don't change. Please? I really like it."

"I'm not sure what to make of this."

"Nothing. Really. I shouldn't have said anything. Except I like it so much. I love to hear you come. Honest."

"Okay, Ronda. I guess I'll believe that you're not making fun of me."

"Not at all."

Ronda sat next to her on the top step and kissed her, softly at first and then harder. She was beginning to get her juices running again after their little disagreement.

"Come on in," she said. "The water's fine."

She swam back out to the center of the pool. She watched Mallory walk down the steps and swim out to join her.

"So I'm a cute comer, huh?"

"Yeah. You really are. And that's nothing to hate me for."

"But I don't know what I do."

"You just come. And that's all you need to do. Now come here."

Ronda wrapped her arms around Mallory and pressed their bodies together. She kissed her full on the mouth and felt her nipples tighten. When the kiss ended, they stayed holding on to each other.

"I guess it's a good thing we're a couple of athletes in great shape," Mallory said.

"No doubt. Normal people would probably have drowned right there."

They frolicked in the pool together. They took turns diving to the bottom of the pool and using the diving board. They were relaxed and easygoing. It was a great evening.

"I have a hot tub, if you're interested," Ronda said.

"Sure," Mallory said. "Let's go turn into prunes."

"Bubbles on or off?"

"Off. I want to see you in the water."

"Fair enough."

They climbed into the warm water. Ronda watched Mallory's breasts float above the water and was sure she'd have to have her again.

"Damn," Mallory said.

"What?"

"As fine and tight as you look normally, you look twice as hot when you're wet."

"Thank you," Ronda said. She slid into the tub and tried to relax. She was keyed up wanting Mallory again.

Mallory climbed into Ronda's lap.

"Well, hello there," Ronda said. She ran her hands up Mallory's thighs.

Mallory leaned in and kissed her hard on the mouth. There was no pretense of gentleness. It was filled with need. Ronda pulled her to her. She pressed their bodies together.

"Damn, woman," she said. "I do like the feel of your body."

"Me, too."

Mallory kissed her again. This time all thoughts left Ronda's mind except pleasing her again. And being pleased by her. She was throbbing and needed release.

She moved her hands farther up Mallory's thighs. Soon they were between her legs. She closed her thumbs over her hard clit.

"Oh, yes," Mallory said. She threw her head back and moved against Ronda's thumbs.

"Oh, God. Oh, Jesus. Oh, yes. Oh, yes. Oh, Ronda. Oh, Ronda!"

Again, Ronda buried her face in Mallory's neck so she couldn't see her smile. She was so damned cute when she came.

"Your turn," Mallory said.

She climbed off Ronda and turned to face her on the shelf. She pried her legs open and ran her fingers over her. She dipped them inside as far as they could go. She stroked her inner walls. Then she moved to her clit.

"That's it, baby," Ronda said. "That's the spot. Oh, yeah. Give it to me. God yes. Oh, yes. Oh, God."

Every muscle in her body tensed until she felt the nerves unwinding and sending light throughout her body. She fought to stay upright in the tub.

"Damn, Mallory. You know how to please me. That's for sure."

"It's fun. I'll admit it. I really like getting you off. Almost as much as I like you getting me off."

"Come on. We should get some sleep. First practice is at eight tomorrow."

❖

The week was good for Ronda. She got through her two practices a day and still managed to show houses that Gayla had scheduled. She sold three houses that week, and she made some killer tackles and got five picks. It was a great week.

She was feeling pretty lucky, so Wednesday night, she called the number on the back of Carleen's business card.

"Hello?" the woman on the other end said.

"Hi. May I speak to Carleen Brynes?"

"Speaking. How may I help you?"

"Hi, Carleen. This is Ronda Meyers."

"Oh, hi, Ronda. To what do I owe this pleasure?"

"I was calling to see if you'd like to go out to dinner Friday night?"

"I'd love it."

"Great. I'll pick you up at seven?"

"Sounds wonderful."

They worked out the details and Ronda sat down with a glass of scotch. Excellent. A date with Carleen. She could still see those sapphire blue eyes staring into hers. She could see the twinkle in them as she accused Ronda of being one of Houston's most eligible bachelorettes.

Yes. They would have fun Friday night. Of this, Ronda was sure.

Friday evening arrived and Ronda was whipped. She had played hard and worked hard and all she wanted to do was go to sleep. Especially because she had practice at ten the next morning and then a showing and then a fundraiser.

But she dressed and sat down with a scotch to mentally prepare herself for her date. She called for a car and waited. When it arrived, she gave the driver the address and off they went. Carleen lived in the Memorial area of Houston. The car pulled up in front of a mammoth two-story house. It covered half a city block. Ronda was impressed.

Ronda knocked on the door and there stood Carleen, looking much more casual than she had at the fundraiser. Of course, Ronda was more casual, as well. Instead of a suit, she was wearing gray slacks and a green golf shirt. Carleen wore a blue pantsuit that showed off her eyes.

"You look great," Ronda said. She bent to kiss her cheek.

"So do you."

"Shall we?" She offered her elbow. Carleen took it and they walked to the car. Ronda held the door while Carleen slid in. She slipped in after her.

"You smell amazing," Carleen said.

"Thanks. It's a cologne I first bought in Jamaica. I found it online when I ran out."

"Jamaica, huh? So, you travel?"

"Yes, ma'am."

"Please don't call me ma'am. I'm already aware I'm old enough to be your mother. I don't need to be reminded."

"Oh, no. I don't think of you as a mother figure at all."

"Well, that's a good thing."

Ronda placed her arm across Carleen's shoulders.

"Nope. Not at all."

Carleen looked up at Ronda and Ronda saw the same yearning in her gaze that she'd seen outside at the museum. She wondered for a moment if she should kiss her. She wasn't sure, but thought Carleen was arching into her. She started to lower her mouth.

"We're here, ma'am," the driver said.

Ronda snapped out of it and sat up straight. Carleen looked down and smoothed out an imaginary wrinkle in her slacks. Ronda climbed out of the car and took Carleen's hand to help her out.

The aromas that hit her nose when they entered the Italian restaurant made Ronda's mouth water.

"My God, it smells good in here," she said.

"It does. It's my favorite Italian restaurant in town."

"I've actually never been here before."

"Well, love, prepare to be impressed."

Love? Ronda wasn't sure she was comfortable with that term of endearment. Especially on the first date. But she reasoned it was just Carleen's way, so let it go.

They approached the maître d' and Ronda gave her name.

"Of course, Ms. Meyers. Your table is ready. Right this way."

Ronda stepped back to let Carleen follow directly behind him. They were stopped twice by people who asked for Ronda's autograph.

When they were finally seated, Ronda apologized.

"I'm sorry. That's always a chance you take."

"Oh, I'm not worried," Carleen said. "I know who I'm out with. I'm patient."

"How patient?" Ronda leaned on her elbows and stared hard at Carleen.

"As patient as I need to be." Carleen casually put her napkin in her lap. Ronda did the same.

The tension between them was palpable. Ronda wished they could blow off dinner and go back to her place. She wanted to see what all Carleen had to offer. But she knew that denying herself Carleen would only make it better when she finally got her. And she planned to have her that night.

"So, what's good here?" Ronda said.

"Anything. I hear the veal parmesan is delicious, but I don't eat veal."

"Neither do I. What do you normally have?"

"I usually get the fettuccine, but I'm sure everything is delicious."

They decided on their meals and sipped wine while they waited.

"So, what's a fundraising pioneer for children do with herself when she's not crusading?" Ronda asked.

Carleen smiled and her eyes twinkled.

"A little of this. A little of that."

"Well, that's a definitive answer."

"Oh, I don't know. I tend to keep myself busy, so I'm never not crusading."

"Well, I'm glad you could take time out of your busy schedule to have dinner with me tonight," Ronda said.

"Oh, the pleasure is all mine, I'm sure."

"We'll see," Ronda said just as the waiter brought their dinner.

After dinner and another bottle of wine, Ronda was feeling quite amorous.

"Shall we have the car drop you off at your house or…" she said as they walked toward the car.

"Is that a classy way of saying 'your place or mine?'"

"I suppose it was."

"Your place would be wonderful," Carleen said.

They sat together in the back of the car. Ronda had her arm around Carleen's shoulders. She realized she had no idea what kind of body Carleen was hiding under her clothes. She always wore loose clothing. And Ronda had certainly never been with anyone her age before. Oh, well, she told herself. She wanted Carleen and was going to have her.

They arrived at the house and Ronda got out and held Carleen's hand to guide her out.

"Wow, Ronda. This is a lovely house," Carleen said.

"Thanks. It's home. Come on in."

She ran her hand down Carleen's back as they walked through the front door. She brought it to rest on her backside. It wasn't the tightest she'd ever felt, but it wasn't bad. Carleen reached around and took her hand.

"There'll be time for that later."

"Sorry."

"Don't be. Just keep the suspense there, love."

Ronda closed the door and turned Carleen to face her. She took her other hand. She looked into Carleen's eyes and saw that same spark. She knew she was wanted. But she felt shy. What was up with that? Ronda was never shy.

She lifted a hand and caressed Carleen's cheek. It was not as smooth as she was used to, but the wrinkles were light. They told of a life well lived. Ronda slipped her hand behind her neck and held her still as she lowered her mouth to taste Carleen's.

She tasted of the wine they had shared. Ronda moved to stand up from the kiss, but Carleen kept her arms wrapped around Ronda's neck. She pulled Ronda back to her and this time, she opened her mouth for Ronda's tongue to enter. Ronda was happy to oblige and felt the tightening in her gut as she became more aroused.

The kiss finally ended.

"What happened to the suspense?" Ronda smiled.

"Don't you worry. We'll keep it going. We'll just expose a little bit at a time."

"You're going to make me crazy."

"That's my goal."

"Fair enough. May I offer you a drink?"

"More wine would be lovely."

"Coming right up. Go ahead and have a seat anywhere you'd like."

She poured Carleen a glass of wine and herself a scotch and then joined Carleen on the couch.

"You really have a beautiful house. Do you have a maid?"

Ronda laughed. She supposed that's what you could call Marie, but she felt more like a housemother to her.

"I have a housekeeper."

"Yes. I can't imagine you'd have time to keep your house up between football and real estate."

"It does get challenging." Ronda was bored with the conversation. She wanted Carleen. But she also knew she wasn't going to have her until she was ready, so she eased back against the couch and rested her hand on Carleen's thigh.

"I have to say, I'm as nervous as a schoolgirl," Carleen said.

"Why's that?"

"I told you before. You're Houston's most eligible bachelorette. And I'm sitting with you here, after dinner. All alone with you in your house."

"Are you uncomfortable?" Ronda said.

"Not really. Just nervous."

"I could always take you home."

"No." She placed her hand over Ronda's. "That won't be necessary. I'm a big girl, Ronda. Ronda. Wow. I still can't believe I'm sitting here with Ronda Meyers. _The_ Ronda Meyers."

"Easy there, Carleen. I'm just me. Don't make me into some superhero."

"But don't you see? For women in Houston especially, you are a hero."

"I don't need that kind of pressure. How about for tonight we're just two women who find each other attractive?"

"It's not going anywhere after tonight, then, is it?"

"I don't know. So far it's been nice. I might like to go out with you again. But I'm not looking for a relationship, if that's what you're asking."

"Fair enough. Besides, you're already in a relationship."

"How do you figure?"

"Gayla Adkins."

"Gayla is my assistant. She takes care of me. We don't have anything extracurricular going on." Ronda knew that wasn't the whole truth, but it was close enough.

"Oh, I think you do. And even if you haven't consummated it, which I doubt, it's still very much there. You two are too in sync. Oh, and don't worry. I'm okay with this because I'm imagining you two haven't set any ground rules yet."

"There are no rules to set. Trust me. I'm not with Gayla."

"Never mind anyway. I want to focus only on us and the way we can make each other feel.

"Now you're talking, Carleen," Ronda said. "Now you're talking."

Chapter Six

Ronda took Carleen's glass of wine and set it on the coffee table. She pulled her close and kissed her softly on her lips. When she tried to pull away, Carleen pulled her back in for a hard, passionate kiss that left Ronda breathless.

"I hope I didn't bruise your lips," Carleen said.

"No. They're fine."

Ronda leaned in and kissed her again. They kissed for what seemed an eternity. And as they kissed, Carleen slid down onto the couch which left Ronda on top of her. She realized it and tried to climb off her.

"No." Carleen held her tight. "Stay where you are."

"I don't want to hurt you."

"You won't."

They kissed some more and Ronda ground her pelvis into Carleen. She was throbbing with need and could feel heat rising from Carleen. She would need more than just this soon. She brought her knee up between Carleen's. Carleen spread her legs wide then closed them over Ronda.

"Oh, shit yes," Ronda said. "Oh, yeah. That's what I'm talking about."

"Mm-hm. This feels amazing."

Ronda kissed down her neck to her chest until she met her blouse. She ran her hand up Carleen's side and closed it around a breast. This elicited a moan from Carleen.

"You like that, huh?" Ronda could hardly breathe. There was so much she wanted to do and she wanted to do it all at one time. She cautioned herself to continue to take it slow. But there was no reason.

Carleen untucked her shirt from her slacks so Ronda could slide her hand under it. She teased her nipple through her bra before lifting the bra over her breast. Her breast just fit in Ronda's hand. And it felt wonderful, but she needed more. She needed to suck, to lick Carleen's nipple and every other body part.

She climbed off her and offered her hand to Carleen.

"Come on. Let's go to bed."

Carleen stood and held tightly to Ronda's hand. They walked into the bedroom. Ronda took Carleen's jacket off and laid it over the chair. She helped her get her blouse off and placed it with her jacket.

"My God, you're beautiful," Ronda said.

"No, my dear. I'm not. I'm not as tight as I used to be. But I'm okay."

"No. You're beautiful."

She took off Carleen's bra and tossed it to the chair. She stood with Carleen's breasts in her hands and kissed her.

Carleen untucked Ronda's shirt and pulled it over her head. Next went the sports bra. She ran her hands over Ronda's muscular chest and shoulders.

"Oh, my God," she said. "You're even more magnificent than I'd dared to dream."

"You're going to make me blush. Now come here."

Ronda pulled her so their skin touched. It was like fireworks shooting off inside her body. She kissed her hard on her mouth before stepping back. She pulled Carleen's slacks down over her ass.

"Sit down," she said.

Carleen sat and Ronda knelt before her. She took her shoes and slacks off. Carleen sat there in her panties. Ronda looked up at her.

"May I take these off?" she said. She stared at her wet crotch and knew Carleen wanted it as badly as she did.

Carleen swallowed hard.

"Please," she said.

Ronda did and stood there taking in the beauty in front of her.

"You're gorgeous," she said. "Lie back."

Carleen lay back on the bed as Ronda finished undressing. She lay with her and ran her hand along her body. She kissed her again. She kissed her neck and chest again and this time licked and sucked a nipple. It was immediately hard for her. She drew it as far into her mouth as she could. She flicked her tongue over it once. Twice. Three times before she kissed farther down her body until she was between her legs.

She kissed her tenderly on each of her inner thighs.

"You smell amazing," she said. She lowered her mouth to taste her. "And you're delicious. Just as I knew you would be."

"It's been a while for me." Carleen was already breathing heavily. "I don't know how long I'll hold out."

"Don't fight it, baby. Let it go."

She continued to lick and suck, and Carleen pressed her face into her while she ground her hips.

She released her death grip.

"Oh, thank you, Ronda. Wow, I needed that."

"There's more where that came from," Ronda said.

"No. I can only have one at a time."

"Maybe I'll be the exception."

"No, you won't. Believe me. I know. Now come up here so I can have at your gorgeous body."

Ronda climbed up next to Carleen. She lay on her back and spread her legs.

"I'm all yours," she said.

"Mm. You are a sight for sore eyes."

"Thank you. Although I do hope you'll do more than just look."

"Oh, yes."

Carleen lay down on top of Ronda and kissed her. She ground herself into her and moaned into her mouth.

She slid off and moved her hand down Ronda's body.

"Damn, you've got a body that just won't quit."

"I'm glad you like it."

"Oh, I do. What's this?" She had her hand rubbing between Ronda's legs. "Someone is very wet."

Ronda grit her teeth. She needed to be fucked, not gently rubbed. She needed more and hoped it was coming soon.

Carleen dipped her fingers inside and stroked her.

"Oh, yeah. That feels so good," Ronda said. "So good."

Carleen withdrew her fingers and rubbed Ronda's clit.

"Oh, shit," Ronda said. "Oh, dear God, yes."

Ronda fought to hold off, but it was no use. The orgasm crashed through her and she relaxed back on the bed.

"May I play some more?" Carleen said.

"Please do."

Carleen plunged her fingers deep inside again. She thrust her fingers in then took them out slowly.

"You like that?" Carleen said.

"Oh, God, yes."

"Mm. You feel so good."

"So do you."

"You're so incredibly wet."

"You've got me very aroused." Ronda felt her rubbing at a very sensitive spot inside. She rotated her hips to make more contact.

"I think I've found a fun spot," Carleen said.

"Oh, yes. Oh, yeah. Please don't stop."

"No way, love. I'm not stopping until you do."

Carleen continued to rub until Ronda cried out. She gave herself over to wave after wave of climax.

"Thank you, Carleen," Ronda said. She pulled Carleen close to her.

"You are so fun," Carleen said.

"As are you. Maybe we can go out again sometime."

"I'd like that."

"Good. So we just need to figure out when."

"Yes. We'll have to work it out between events and such."

"And the season starts for me in a few weeks, which will mean less time to date."

"Well, I won't pin you down. That's not my intention."

"And I appreciate that."

"So, my darling, Ronda. It is time for me to go home."

"What? You're not going to stay here?"

"I need to go. Please understand. I don't spend the night away from home."

"Okay. Let me drive you home."

The next day, Ronda practiced hard. She put herself through the paces to make herself faster and stronger. She intercepted two passes and made several tackles. Including one of Mallory.

She helped her up off the field and patted her ass. Mallory shot her a look that she couldn't read through her mask. She hoped it was a smile.

After practice she showered and headed off to Chapman Lake Court to meet Gayla for her showing. Gayla was waiting for her when she arrived.

"Why do we schedule showings on days when I have practice and a fundraiser?" she asked.

"To keep you off the streets."

"Funny."

"Anyway, here's the information on the house and the buyers."

Ronda studied the information and was ready when the Bremers showed up. She introduced herself to them and showed them around the house. They fell in love and Ronda went over the price, which she knew they could afford. They made an offer and Ronda could cross one more responsibility off her list for the day.

"How about a drink?" Ronda said.

"Do we have time?"

"We have two hours before your big fundraiser."

"Yes, but it's my fundraiser tonight. I'm throwing it to raise money for the team. I need to be there early. So I'll have to take a raincheck on the drink."

"Bummer, but okay. I should go home and rest for a while anyway."

Ronda was fidgety when she got home. She was dreading the event, as usual. And this time Gayla was the chair so she wouldn't even have her to hang around with. Then she remembered that since it was a fundraiser for the team itself, members of the team would be there. That would be cool. Maybe she would have a good time, after all.

She relaxed with a drink out by the pool until it was seven o'clock, when the gig started. She finished her drink and called for the car. It got there at seven fifteen, which meant she'd arrive fashionably late, and that worked for her.

When she got out of the car, flashes went off and several people thrust footballs in her hands, asking for autographs. She smiled and signed and shook hands before walking into the venue.

The room was packed. It was shoulder to shoulder throughout. Ronda pushed through looking for Gayla. She grabbed a glass of champagne and stood there, sipping and looking. She felt a light touch on her elbow.

"Hello, Ronda."

"Hello, Carleen. I guess I should have expected to see you tonight."

"Oh, yes. I wouldn't have missed this."

"You look great," Ronda said. Carleen was wearing another blue slack suit. It complemented her eyes perfectly.

"Thank you. So do you. You look positively delicious."

Ronda winked at her.

A woman came up then and wrapped her arm around Carleen.

"Shall we mingle, my love?" the woman said.

"Yes, dear. Let's. Excuse us," she said to Ronda as she allowed the woman to escort her away. Ronda thought it was odd that she didn't even warrant an introduction. And what about their terms of endearment? Was Carleen in a committed relationship? Ronda shook her head. She knew nothing about the woman, obviously. The thought struck her as odd, though.

She pressed on through the crowd and came to Mallory, all dressed up in a black suit with a green shirt underneath.

"Wow," Ronda said. "You sure clean up nice."

Mallory laughed.

"You don't look so bad yourself."

As Ronda stood there, Canfield walked up with two glasses of champagne and handed one to Mallory. Obviously, they'd made up. That made Ronda very happy. Mallory seemed to have a lot of talent and Ronda wanted to see her get as much playing time as possible.

"What's up, Canfield?" Ronda said.

"Not much. How you doin'?"

"Oh, you know. I'm surviving. These things can be such a drag."

"I think they're pretty cool," Canfield said. "People all asking for your autograph and stuff."

"I'm too new for that," Mallory said. "I'm mostly here for the champagne."

They all laughed. Then Gayla's voice could be heard throughout the room. She had a microphone on a platform at the front of the room. She called for all the members of the Stars who were there to please come up to the front of the room.

There were twenty members of the team who had shown up for the event. She introduced them to the crowd, one at a time. When she got to Mallory, she introduced her.

"The future of the Stars' running game," she said.

Ronda was introduced last.

"Ladies and gentlemen, the pride of Houston Stars football. Last year's league MVP. I give you Ronda Meyers."

The crowd went crazy. Cheers erupted and went on for several minutes. Ronda stepped forward, smiled brightly, and waved to the crowd. They loved her and she really appreciated it. They were who she practiced hard for every day and played her ass off for every Saturday during the season.

When the applause died down, they walked off the platform. All, but Ronda, who stayed behind to talk to Gayla.

"You look great, babe," she said. "How is tonight going?"

"So far, so good. You look amazing, too. Wow, did you hear those cheers you got? Your fans adore you."

"I consider them my bosses in a way, you know?" Ronda said. "They're the ones paying my salary by filling those seats to watch me play. I'm glad they like me."

"What's not to like, anyway?" Gayla said.

"Thank you. You're too kind. Well, I suppose I should go mingle."

"You're not bugging out early?"

"I thought I'd make it through the whole gig and then help you close down, if that's okay."

"That would be wonderful. Thank you."

Ronda stepped off the platform and mingled with the masses. She signed footballs, jerseys, posters, even cocktail napkins. The night was fun, but soon, she was dragging. She thought about finding Gayla and begging off from helping her close down when she heard her voice over the loudspeaker.

"Thank you very much all of you who came tonight to help support our Stars. We'd like to especially thank the members of the team who could be here to help us out." The crowd exploded in applause. "We'll see you all when the season starts in three weeks."

The people started filing out then, right on cue. Ronda stood back by the table where people deposited empty champagne glasses. She thanked everyone for coming. Finally, the place was empty save the serving staff and Gayla and Ronda.

"So, what now?" Ronda said.

"We're through. The cost of cleanup came with the with rental cost. So, we leave them to do their things and we take off."

"Oh, thank God. I didn't know how much longer I'd last."

"I know. I'm beat."

Ronda draped her arm across Gayla's shoulders.

"Do you need a ride home?"

"That would be great."

"Or you could come to my place."

"I'm sorry, Ronda. Tempting though that is, I'm beat."

"Yes, but you cleared my schedule for tomorrow, right?"

"Right."

"So, come spend the night with me and we'll find something to do tomorrow," Ronda said.

"Just sleep tonight, though? You promise?"

"I promise."

"Okay, baby. That sounds great."

Chapter Seven

They got back to Ronda's and went straight to bed. They lay there naked and Ronda had to remind herself that she was exhausted. It just felt so right having Gayla with her. She wanted to claim her.

"Can I ask you a question?" Gayla said.

"Sure."

"Why are you so afraid of commitment?"

"Oh, wow. We're gonna get all deep and dark now? At this hour?"

"Come on. And don't feed me any bullshit. I mean, I know you enjoy playing around. Who doesn't? But for you, there seems to be a real fear of commitment and I just wanted to know why?"

"So, everyone likes to play the field?" Ronda said.

"Well, not everyone I suppose. But a lot of people do."

"You want the truth?"

"I'd love the truth."

Ronda propped herself on an elbow and looked down into Gayla's eyes.

"Suppose I had a woman. And we were in love and life was good."

"Yeah?"

"And suppose I get traded. Then what? I move to a new city and I deal with leaving my woman behind and it hurts and I don't want to go through that."

"You fool." She slapped Ronda's arm playfully. "Your woman would go with you."

"I would never ask her to. I would never uproot a woman from her life here and ask her to go with me. That's plain selfish. And I wouldn't be able to take the pain of leaving her behind."

"I call bullshit. That's a chicken shit excuse." She rolled over so her back was to Ronda.

"Babe, I'm telling the truth." She ran her hand down Gayla's arm. "It's my greatest fear."

Gayla rolled back over.

"You're serious, aren't you?"

"I am."

"Wow."

"I like to think the Stars won't trade me and I'll retire here, but I don't know that. I'll never know that for sure. I mean for now, I'm their golden girl, but what about next season or the season after that?"

"How much longer do you plan on playing, Ronda? This is already season number seven."

"I want to play twelve seasons. The likelihood of them all being here is between slim and none."

"Okay. At least I get why you shy away from commitment now."

"What is this all about anyway?"

"I was just curious,"

"Are you sure?" Ronda said.

"I'm sure."

They rolled over and spooned. Ronda held Gayla tight all night. She awoke the next morning to an empty bed, but the smell of coffee. She smiled. Gayla walked in holding two cups of coffee.

"I wondered if you were ever going to wake up," she said.

"What time is it?" Ronda sat up and accepted a cup of coffee.

"It's nine."

"Wow. I must have been tired."

"I guess so. That conversation we had last night must have really drained you."

"Very funny. How long have you been up?"

"About an hour."

"Yeah? What have you been doing?"

"Reading the paper, making coffee, just enjoying the morning."

"Well," Ronda said. "Why don't you set your coffee down and climb back into bed so we can enjoy the morning a little more?"

"I thought you'd never ask." She shed her white robe and slipped into bed.

Ronda kissed down Gayla's body, stopping to play with her nipples. She sucked one and then the other before continuing her way downward. She spread Gayla's legs and licked her. She lapped at her opening before sucking her clit and flicking her tongue over it. That always did the trick and soon Gayla came for her.

Ronda flipped Gayla over and pulled her up on all fours. She buried her face between her legs while she reached around and stroked her clit. Again, the orgasms were almost instantaneous.

Gayla collapsed on the bed and rolled over.

"What was that all about?"

"What?" Ronda said.

"In all the times we've had sex, you've never taken me that way."

"I was in the mood for something different. Didn't you enjoy it?"

"Very much."

"Okay, then."

"And now it's your turn, my ebony stud."

"Knock yourself out."

Ronda spread her legs for Gayla. She felt Gayla running her hands all over her body.

"I can't get over how tight your body is," Gayla said. "I love the muscles that ripple when I touch you."

"Good. I work hard to get those muscles."

"I know you do. I just want you to know I appreciate them."

She dragged her hand between Ronda's legs and plunged her fingers inside. She took them out before thrusting them back in.

"More," Ronda said. "I need more."

"You got it. Here's more."

Ronda could feel herself filled more to her liking. She ground her hips in rhythm to the thrusting to make Gayla's fingers touch all her sensitive spots. She was close to coming, but needed her clit touched. She reached down and rubbed it while Gayla continued to move in and out.

She closed her eyes as tight as she could and focused only on the sensations between her legs. It was only a matter of minutes before one orgasm after another washed over her body.

"We're a good team," she said.

"Yes, we are."

They lay there for a little while, not saying anything, simply cuddling. It felt good to Ronda to be able to do that. Gayla finally needed to get up.

"We can't lie in bed all day," she said.

"Sure we can." Ronda closed a long arm around her and pulled her closer.

"No, we can't. We've got coffee to drink and gossip to talk about."

"Gossip?" Ronda propped herself up on one elbow. "Now I'm intrigued."

"So, get up."

Gayla got up and put her robe back on. She handed one to Ronda. They took their coffee into the kitchen for warm-ups then sat at the kitchen table.

"So, spill," Ronda said.

"Well, do you remember at last week's fundraiser I walked out onto the patio just as Carleen Brynes was getting ready to kiss you?"

"I don't think we established that's what was happening, but I do remember."

"Well, apparently, you're not the only celebrity in town she's hit on."

"That doesn't matter to me, Gayla. You've got to know that."

"No, I know. But I did find it interesting that she was at last night's event with her partner of twenty-five years."

"No way!" Ronda wasn't sure what to feel. She felt like she'd been totally used by Carleen, but that normally wouldn't bother her.

The fact that Carleen had a partner made it feel dirty. She decided to cross her off her bedmate list.

"Oh, my God," Gayla said.

"What?"

"You've slept with her."

"What? No."

"Don't you lie to me, Ronda Meyers. I can read you like a book. I can totally see it on your face. You've fucked her."

Ronda looked down into her coffee.

"Yeah, I did. But to be fair, I didn't know about her partner."

"She's way older than you, too."

"Hey, let's not get into age differences, sunshine."

"I'm not *that* much older than you," Gayla said.

"True. Anyway, don't worry. I won't be going to bed with her again."

"Good." Gayla shuddered. "That's just gross."

"Do you have any other gossip?" Ronda asked. She thought about seeing Canfield with Mallory the previous night.

"Nope. That was all the talk was. What a whore Carleen is. I'm telling you, at least half the conversations going on last night were about that."

"I wonder why she brought her partner last night."

"Apparently, she's a huge Stars fan. You, in particular."

"Oh, that makes me feel better." Ronda couldn't help the sarcasm.

"Now see," Gayla said, "if you would just settle down, you wouldn't need to worry about this kind of thing."

"No, instead I'd be wondering if I was ever getting sex again."

"What's that supposed to mean?" Gayla said.

"You know how relationships are. It's all groovy in the beginning but then slowly she gets tired of sex and now you're trapped and you're not allowed to go get any stray stuff so you're stuck."

"Well, obviously you'd settle down with someone who has the same sexual appetite you do."

"You make it all sound so simple. But it's not."

"I think it is. I think you're afraid."

"I am afraid. I told you that last night. I'm afraid of getting hurt or of hurting someone else. I couldn't handle it. For now, I've got my careers to focus on."

"And you have me."

"What?"

"You have me. I take care of you. I sleep with you. I do everything a wife would do."

"Look, Gayla, we've talked about this."

"I'm just saying. I make it easy for you to stay free and single."

Ronda thought hard about what Gayla said. She had a point. But what was she really trying to say? Did she want to be Ronda's wife?

"What?" Gayla said. "You can't deny that I do that. You can go do whatever you want because you know I'm going to make sure you're where you need to be when you need to be there."

"A wife does so much more than that."

"True. I'm not saying I'm your wife. I'm saying I make it easy for you to remain single."

"You may be right."

"I am right."

"I'm tired of this conversation. Let's go for a swim."

The pool felt good. It was nice to be out of the humidity and swimming around. Ronda relaxed with her back against the wall and watched Gayla swim laps. She was trim and lovely to watch cut through the water. She pulled up at the shallow end and sat on the steps.

"Are you going to swim?" she said.

"Maybe. Or maybe I'll relax here all day."

"You look good there." She swam over and placed one hand on either side of Ronda's head. She kissed her lightly on her lips, then her cheek, then her earlobe. "And you taste like chlorine."

"Sorry about that." Ronda laughed.

"No. I don't mind."

"Good. Then kiss away."

Gayla kissed back to Ronda's lips and sucked them.

"I love your lips," she said.

"I love what you do to them," Ronda said.

"I love what you do with them." Gayla smiled.

"Why don't you climb out of the pool and we'll see what I can do with them?"

Gayla climbed out and sat on the edge of the pool. Ronda spread her legs and held on to her thighs.

"You're beautiful. Do you know that?"

"I'm glad you think so."

"God, do I ever."

Ronda slowly dragged her tongue over Gayla. She dipped it inside and swirled it along her walls. She moved it back to her clit and brought her to an orgasm that caused her body to tremble.

"Why, thank you," Gayla said. "I needed that."

"You're welcome. Now, I'm hungry. Let's go get something to eat."

"Baby, the only clothes I have here are the clothes I wore over last night. I'll need to take a shower and get a change of clothes."

"Fine. We'll take a shower, and then I'll take you to get a change of clothes."

They got in the shower, and this time it was Gayla who took charge. She pressed Ronda against the wall and kissed her while her fingers found her hard clit. She stroked it until Ronda had to hold on to Gayla to keep her balance as she came.

They finished their showers and dried off.

"Do you just want to wear one of my robes or do you want to get all dolled up again just to go home and change?" Ronda said.

"I'll put on my clothes. I'd look ridiculous walking in wearing one of your robes."

"Okay. Suit yourself."

They got in Ronda's truck and she drove Gayla home to change. It was eleven o'clock when they finally arrived at the restaurant. While waiting to be seated, several people came up to ask Ronda for her autograph. She happily obliged.

They were finally seated and Gayla's face went pale.

"What?" Ronda said.

"Don't look now, but Carleen Brynes is here with Canfield."

"Oh, my God. That's hilarious."

"That woman gets around," Gayla said. "I sure hope you didn't catch anything from her. If you give me anything, so help me God."

"Don't worry." Although Ronda did worry. She could easily have caught something from Carleen.

"You know, we haven't talked about this in a long time, but you really need to use protection as much as you sleep around."

Ronda took a deep breath and blew it out her mouth.

"Look, Gayla, I really don't sleep around as much as you think I do."

"I beg to differ."

"I don't. I don't have time. You know that."

"It's true I keep you busy, but I give you a few minutes unattended and you're sleeping with a slut like Carleen."

"True. I'm guilty of that indiscretion, but for the most part, I'm keeping it in my pants."

"For the most part huh?"

"Yeah."

"I'm not asking. I don't want details. I'm just asking you to please be careful."

"Yes, ma'am. Now relax and enjoy brunch."

Chapter Eight

They were just finishing up their brunch when Canfield and Carleen walked up.

"Hey, you two," Canfield said. "I just wanted to thank you for all the hard work you put in for last night's event, Gayla. It turned out really well."

"Thank you. I was happy with the turnout."

"Well, we'd better get going. Just wanted to thank you."

As they walked off, Carleen dragged her arm across Ronda's shoulders.

"Ew," Gayla whispered. "Just ew."

"Yeah. That was pretty gross."

"Okay, we're running an errand before we go home."

"And by home, where do you mean?"

"I thought we'd go back to your place and hang out for the day. Is that okay?"

"Sure. No problem."

Ronda was actually excited about spending more time with Gayla. She was so easy to be with. And she had no expectations, which was nice.

They left the restaurant and Gayla pulled up an address on her phone.

"It's on Richmond. Get on the freeway here," Gayla said.

"Do you mind telling me where we're going?"

"Yes, I do mind. If I told you, you wouldn't go. This way, at least we'll get there. Then I just need to convince you to go inside."

They followed Gayla's directions and Ronda pulled into the parking lot of Madame Eve's.

"You're fucking kidding me," Ronda said. "A sex shop?"

"You're buying some dental dams. And you're going to use them."

"Oh, shit. I don't know, Gayla…"

"I do know. I'm tired of taking chances."

Ronda wanted to tell her that she was one of a handful of women she slept with, but kind of liked the reputation she had of being a player.

Gayla climbed out of the truck and stood there waiting for Ronda. Ronda finally climbed out and walked over next to Gayla.

"If anybody recognizes me here, you're dead meat," Ronda said.

"Who's going to recognize you? Look around, Ronda. The parking lot is empty."

"Okay. Fine. Let's go get some dental dams."

Ronda stepped inside and felt like she was in a sex toy supermarket. There were rows and rows of toys of any variety she could imagine.

They walked up to the help desk.

"Do you have dental dams?" Gayla asked.

"Dude! You're that football player, aren't you?" The young woman behind the counter was wide-eyed as she looked at Ronda.

"Yes." Ronda smiled. "Yes, I am."

"Wow. And you're here. In this store on my shift. Holy shit. I'm a huge fan."

"Thank you."

"Now, about those dental dams?" Gayla said.

"Oh, yeah, safe sex," the girl behind the counter said.

She pointed them in the direction of the dams and Gayla and Ronda set off. Ronda stopped every few feet and asked Gayla if she thought this toy looked fun or if she'd like to try that toy. There were so many and Ronda wanted to buy one of everything.

"Would you please focus?" Gayla said.

"I can't."

"Choose a flavor. What's your favorite?"

"I don't know. I guess I should choose cherry, right? Doesn't that make sense?"

"You're horrible, but okay. We'll get you cherry. Now let's get out of here."

"Wait. I want some new toys."

"Oh, come on, Ronda. Order them online, like any other respectable human."

"No can do. These look fun."

She grabbed three toys and the dams and paid with cash.

They left the store just as a few more cars pulled into the parking lot.

"I'm sure she called some friends to come see you were in her store."

"You think?"

"I do."

"Oh, well, their loss. We got out of there before they got there."

"So, what on earth did you buy?"

Gayla went through the bag.

"Just some things," Ronda said.

"What is *this*?" Gayla pulled out a black, almost U-shaped toy.

"It's a strapless strap-on. Check it out. This part goes inside me and that part goes inside my partner. And it vibrates. How fun is that?"

"Maybe we should have bought condoms, too."

"What? Now you're talking nonsense. I'll wash it after every use. It's waterproof."

"Okay. If you say so."

"Well, you know I've never used it before, so it's clean right, now?"

"Yeah, so?"

"So, I was thinking we could take it for a test run when we got home."

"Oh, you were, were you?"

"Sure, why not?" Ronda said.

"You think I'm that easy?"

"I think you like sex as much as I do, and we always enjoy it together, so why not enjoy it together with a new toy?"

"Fine. But I want to drive."

"No, you don't," Ronda said.

Gayla laughed.

"You're right. I don't want to drive. At least not the first few times."

"Good. Glad we got that settled."

They arrived back at the house and Ronda held the door open for Gayla. As soon as she closed it, she pressed Gayla into it and kissed her hard on her mouth, begging for entry with her tongue.

Gayla opened her mouth and welcomed Ronda. She wrapped her arms around her neck and pulled her closer. Ronda grabbed her ass and pulled their pelvises together. She ground into Gayla. She loved the familiar feel of their bodies together.

Ronda broke the kiss and leaned her forehead on Gayla's. She was breathing heavily, and every inch of her was bursting with need.

"I've got to have you, baby," she said.

"Then take me."

Ronda took the bag of toys from Gayla and they walked into the bedroom. Ronda kissed Gayla again as she stripped her, then herself. Gayla lay on the bed while Ronda stood there, attempting to open the package the toy was in. She was fighting with it and was not amused. The fact that she was shaking with desire didn't help to get the package open.

Gayla lay back on the bed, teasing herself while she watched Ronda.

"Problem, stud?" she said.

"You're not helping."

"But it feels oh so good."

"Shit! Why won't this damned package open?"

She bit the corner and finally got it to tear slightly. She ripped it further and tore the toy out.

"Oh, my God. I didn't think that was ever coming out," Ronda said.

"Hurry up, baby. I don't think I can wait long."

"Okay. Let's see how this works. I'll slide it in me first."

"Turn it on first," Gayla said.

"Oh, yeah. Right. Turn it on. Oh, my God, this thing's got some force. Now I'll slide it in me."

She slid her end in and grabbed hold of it. She positioned herself above Gayla and together they got the other end inside her.

"Oh, yeah," Gayla said. "Oh, that's nice."

Ronda switched it so the toy pulsated.

"What do you think of that?"

"Holy fuck. That's amazing."

Ronda lay on top of Gayla and kissed her hard on her mouth while she relished their bodies touching while the toy fucked them both.

"Oh, my God. This is awesome," she said as she kissed Gayla's neck.

"Tell me about it." Gayla wrapped her legs around Ronda's hips.

Ronda rocked against her, driving the toy deeper inside her.

"I can't take much more," Gayla said.

"Let it go, babe," Ronda said. "Let go for me."

Gayla threw her head back and cried out as orgasm after orgasm coursed through her body.

Ronda gave herself permission to come and held tight to Gayla as she climaxed one, two, three times.

"Holy shit," she said. She turned off the toy. "That was fucking amazing."

She withdrew the toy from inside her and rolled off Gayla. She slowly slid the other end out of her.

"Wow," Gayla said. "Just wow."

"I know, right? Who knew how much fun that would be? And you thought I was crazy for buying toys."

"Well, now I want to see what other toys you bought," Gayla said.

"Not right now. I can't take any more right now." She rolled over and pulled Gayla to her in a warm embrace.

"Mm. That's nice," Gayla said.

"Sh. Just go to sleep now. We'll play more later."

They awoke two hours later.

"Wow," Ronda said. "We were wiped out."

"I don't know if I've ever had as powerful orgasms as I had with that toy. Nothing personal."

"No. No worries. That thing rocked me to my very core, as well."

"I'm so glad you bought it. Now, are you going to show me what else you bought?"

"All in due time, babe. All in due time. Now, I was contemplating grillin' a couple of steaks. How does that sound?"

"Oh, my God. After the brunch we had? I don't think I should."

"Well, I'd feel weird eating in front of you, but I'm hungry."

"How about this, you eat a steak and a salad and I eat a salad?"

"That sounds great."

They donned robes and Ronda worked the grill while Gayla made the salad. They sat on the deck and ate.

"I should probably get going," Gayla said after they'd cleaned up the dishes.

"Nonsense. The evening is still young. Let's enjoy the hot tub."

"That sounds wonderful."

They climbed in the tub and soaked for a few minutes.

"That's what I'm talkin' about," Ronda said.

"Yes. It is very nice, but I still should get going."

"What's your hurry?"

"I don't know. I just feel like I've been here too long. I don't want to overstay my welcome, you know."

"You're fine. Just relax."

"Okay. If you say so."

"I say so."

Ronda reached out of the tub and took something out of the pocket of her robe.

"What's that?" Gayla said.

"It's yet another toy."

"Oh, jeez. I don't know if I can take another toy."

"You're going to love this. Trust me."

She managed to get it out of its package. It was a doughnut-looking toy.

"That doesn't look like much fun," Gayla said.

"Oh, ye of little faith. You just spread those legs and we'll see how fun it is."

"What's it supposed to do?"

"It's supposed to replicate oral sex. Only by like a professional."

"Baby, you know you rock my world. I doubt this toy can do me any better."

"Well, let's try."

She placed the toy between Gayla's legs and pressed the control button.

"Oh, wow," Gayla said. "That's nice."

"Just nice?"

"Yeah, it feels good."

Ronda adjusted the control.

"Oh." Gayla spread her legs wider and sat up straighter. "Oh, my."

"Yeah?"

"Oh, yeah."

Ronda adjusted the controls again and this time Gayla closed her eyes.

"Oh, yes. Oh, God, yes. Oh, please. Don't stop."

Ronda moved the toy slowly from one end to another and back again.

"Oh, baby. Oh, shit. That feels so good."

"Come for me, Gayla. Show me how good it feels."

"Oh, dear God, baby. Oh, sweet Jesus." She reached down and grabbed Ronda's wrist. "Oh, yeah, baby. Don't stop."

"I'm not going to. Tell me what you need."

"Just keep doing what you're doing."

Ronda didn't believe her. She thought she needed something different to get her off, so she switched the controls again.

"Oh, Ronda!" Gayla cried out as she came. "Oh, my God. That was amazing."

"Yeah? Good to know."

"No way. You're not just going to take my word for it. You're going to try it out."

"I'm good, Gayla. Thanks though."

"Please? It's really something else, Ronda."

"Okay." She explained to Gayla how to use the controller.

"That explains it," Gayla said. "You were controlling swirls, licks, and flicks."

Ronda smiled.

"Guilty as charged."

"Well, now you spread those gorgeous legs of yours and let me at you."

Ronda happily obliged. She spread her legs as wide as she could and relaxed while Gayla familiarized herself with the toy. When Gayla touched it to Ronda's clit, she jumped.

"Oh, wow," Ronda said.

"See?"

"Oh, yeah."

Gayla adjusted the controls.

"Holy shit, Gayla. Oh, God. That's perfect. Oh, shit. Oh, yes." She tensed up and then relaxed, feeling relieved after the orgasms had washed over her. "Damn, Gayla."

"I told you. That toy is out of control."

"Yeah, it is. It's fuckin' amazing."

Ronda took the toy from Gayla and put it back in the pocket of her robe.

"Dare I ask what else you bought?" Gayla said.

"Nothing major. It's just for fun. We'll use it at bedtime tonight."

"So I'm staying the night? That's good to know."

"Why wouldn't you?" Ronda asked. "Do you have somewhere to go?"

"No. I have no plans. It's Sunday night, for crying out loud. Who does anything on a Sunday night?"

"Speaking of it being Sunday night, we should probably go over my schedule for the week.

"Well, since Coach only has you down for one practice a day, I thought I'd load up your afternoons with showings."

"Good. Let's make some money this week."

"That would be the plan."

Ronda nuzzled Gayla's neck.

"You taste so good."

"I'm turning into a prune."

"Aw. Does that mean we've got to get out?"

"Yes, it does."

They got out and were drying off.

"Hey," Ronda said. "Do I have anything going on Saturday night?"

"Sorry, hon. You've got a political fundraiser Friday night and a medical center gig Saturday."

"Oh, man. Those sound thrilling. Not."

"Why? Were you planning on doing something Saturday?"

"No. Just hoping for a night off. Will I ever have one?"

"Sure. As soon as the season starts. You'll play games on Saturday and I promise not to set you up with any commitments Saturday nights."

"Well, thank God for that."

"Are you sure you don't want to take me home?" Gayla asked.

"Look, if you don't want to stay, you don't have to. But I'd like for you to. You said you have nothing going on."

"No, not for my sake. I'm fine with it. But I thought you'd want to have your place to yourself. You're not one for repeat performances."

"But I'm in the mood for one tonight. It's been a fun twenty-four hours, hasn't it?"

"It really has."

"Great," Ronda said. She pulled Gayla to her "Then let's get to bed."

"Right now?" Gayla placed her hands on Ronda's chest.

"Yes. I want you right now."

"Mm. Lead the way."

Ronda took Gayla's hand and led her to the bedroom. She reached into her bag from the toy store and pulled out one more item. She set it on the bedside table.

"Are you going to tell me what it is?" Gayla said.

"Not yet. You'll see soon enough."

She climbed on top of Gayla and kissed her. She felt the kiss deep in her center. There was something powerful about Gayla's kisses. Ronda couldn't get enough of them. Sure, she had kissed her fair share of women in her life, but none of them compared to Gayla.

She ground her hips into Gayla, who wrapped her legs around her. Ronda kissed down Gayla's neck and chest until she got to her breasts. She sucked one and then the other.

"Oh, yes," Gayla said. "That feels so good."

Ronda rolled off of her and, with shaky hands, tried to open the third toy package.

"Do you need help?" Gayla was out of breath.

"No. I got it." She wasn't sure how true that was, but she was determined to try. She finally ripped the package open and took out a funky shaped toy. It was another U-shaped toy, but this time the U was practically closed.

"How does this one work?" Gayla said.

"Apparently, this longer end goes inside you and the slightly shorter, thinner one goes outside against your lips and clit."

"It looks like it would be painful."

"It's supposed to be wonderful. Now, come on, baby. Spread those legs for me."

Ronda guided the toy inside Gayla. She gently placed the outer piece against her sensitive spots.

"Oh, yeah. That feels good," Gayla said. "That's really awesome."

"Good, baby. What do I need to do differently?"

"Nothing. Nothing at all. Just keep it where it is. Oh, God, Ronda."

"Yeah? You like it? It feels good? Show me. Show me, Gayla. Come for me, babe."

"Oh, shit, Ronda. I'm gonna come. Oh, God yes. Oh, God yes."

She pulled Ronda to her and held her close as she rode out the orgasms.

CHAPTER NINE

Monday morning came way too early for Ronda. She wanted to sleep some more but knew she had to take Gayla home and then get to practice. At least they only had one practice a day now that the season was so close.

She got to the gym early and got started lifting. She was almost halfway through with her routine when the rest of the team showed up. They moved through their rotations until Coach Poehl came in and gathered them for their meeting.

Ronda sat in the front so she wouldn't miss anything. She took in everything Coach had to say. Then they watched films of Saturday's practice. Ronda sat forward, elbows on knees, and watched every play she was in. Could she have made her hits faster, harder? There were a few passes she could have picked, she thought. She needed to work on her timing.

By the time they were through watching the films, Ronda was itching to get onto the field. She lined up and waited for the offense to call the play. It was a lateral to Mallory. She broke through the line and tried to move away from Ronda, but Ronda tackled her. Hard.

She helped her up.

"You okay?"

"Sure."

"Good. No hard feelings?"

"None."

That was awkward, Ronda thought, then pushed it out of her head and readied herself for the next play.

Coach Hindley pulled her out at halftime.

"You've played enough today. I don't want to see any injuries. Now, go hit the bath and then the showers."

Ronda soaked in ice until her trainer told her she'd had enough. Then she hit the shower and dressed. She walked back onto the field to catch the rest of the scrimmage. She noticed Mallory was sitting on the bench.

"That was some run you made earlier," Ronda said.

"I want the job. I've got to do my best."

"I guess you want it. That was fairly obvious."

"Good. Now if only the coaches can see it."

"I'm sure they can. Hey, you want to grab a bite to eat tonight?"

"Um, I don't know."

"What? What's up?" Ronda was dying to know if she was seeing Canfield.

"I'm kind of seeing someone now."

"Very cool. Anybody I know?"

"I'd rather not talk about it," Mallory said.

"Fair enough. Well, good luck."

Ronda walked down the sideline and stood next to Coach Hindley. She pointed out areas she thought they could tighten up and what areas looked sharp. She and Coach chatted while the players moved off the field. Practice was over.

Ronda glanced at her watch. Her first showing was in an hour. She'd better hurry up to make it with enough time to keep Gayla happy. Ronda grinned to herself as she crossed the parking lot to her car. So Canfield and Mallory were seeing each other, huh? Well, what about seeing Canfield with Carleen? That didn't make any sense. She'd have to dig deeper, but not now. She had work to do.

As she drove to the house she was showing, she thought about what Mallory dating Canfield really meant to her. It wasn't a no biggie. It was significant. Now that she'd crossed Carleen off her sleep partner list, Mallory and Gayla were all she had left. If Mallory wasn't available, what was Ronda going to do? She'd have to get out and meet some people. And soon.

After the showings, she told Gayla she had someplace to be. It wasn't exactly a lie. She did have to meet people and she figured a bar might be a good idea. She decided to check the clubs to see which ones might be hopping on a Monday night. Though she didn't hold out much hope. She kept her fingers crossed. She wanted to meet someone new. She just had to. She needed a repertoire. How had she ended up with only one playmate?

She went home and changed her slacks and donned a white button-down long sleeved shirt. She left it open at the collar and put on her lucky gold chain. She spritzed on a bit of cologne and called it good. She was ready to seduce some poor, unsuspecting hotty.

She laughed. She would be lucky to find a hotty on a Monday night, but she had to try. She went to The V, a popular lesbian club. She walked in and let her eyes adjust to the darkness. The place was empty. Maybe it was too early. She crossed over to the bar and ordered a bourbon on the rocks.

"So, is this place gonna pick up at all, or am I looking at a typical Monday night?" Ronda asked the bartender.

"You're looking at typical Monday night. We might get a handful of people, but not many people come in."

"Bummer. Where does everyone go on a Monday night?"

"Home to rest up after their weekend and to start planning their Friday nights."

"Yeah. That's kind of what I was afraid of."

"I mean, you can check Rizzo's, but I don't think you'll have much more luck there."

"Maybe I will. Thanks."

Ronda finished her drink and left the bar. She sat in her truck contemplating going home. She wanted to check out Rizzo's, but knew it would be dead as well. She wished she had Friday night off so she could make the rounds and meet someone. She went home and went to bed, discouraged.

The next day was a repeat of the day before. Practice and showings. She said good night to Gayla and drove to Rizzo's. She just thought she'd take a chance and see if anything was going on. The parking lot was crowded. That was a good sign. She walked in and saw the place was packed. She walked up to the bar and ordered her drink.

"I didn't expect this place to be so crowded on a Tuesday night."

"It's Trivia Night," the bartender said. "We always get a good crowd for it. If you want to play and don't have a team, you can go sit over there."

She motioned to a table against the wall.

"If a team needs a substitute player, they call someone from that table."

"Good to know. Thanks."

Ronda took her drink over to the table. She didn't really want to get picked for a team, but she noticed a couple of nice looking ladies sitting there. She sat down.

"I'm Ronda," she said to the table in general.

A few women shook her hand. One stood up and screamed.

"Oh, my God! You're Ronda Meyers!"

Ronda looked around to make sure the whole bar wasn't staring at her. They weren't, so she simply shook the nice looking lady's hand.

"Yes. I'm Ronda Meyers. And who might you be?"

"I'm Miranda. Oh, my God. It's so amazing. I can't believe you're here. I'm a huge fan."

"Well, thank you, Miranda. Can I buy you a drink?"

"Oh, I don't drink. But thank you."

"So you a big fan of the Stars?" Ronda said.

"Huge," Miranda said. "Like mondo fan."

"That's great. I love to meet new fans."

"Oh, my God. I can't believe you're sitting here. Do you mind if I get a picture with you?"

"Not at all."

Ronda draped her arm across Miranda's shoulders while they had another woman at the table take their picture.

"Thank you," Miranda said. "Thank you so much."

"My pleasure. So do you come here every Tuesday?"

"Not every Tuesday. We used to have a team and we'd come, but the team broke up so I only come once in a while in case someone needs an extra player."

"Okay. Do you get picked often?"

"It's hit and miss. But I don't mind just watching and guessing the answers in my head. You've never been here before have you?"

Ronda shook her head.

"I didn't think so. I'd totally remember you."

Ronda smiled.

"You're really good for my ego."

Miranda blushed.

"Good."

"You sure you don't want something to drink? A lemonade? Something?"

"No, thank you. I'm fine."

Ronda felt weird. She knew she could take Miranda home and have her eight ways to Sunday, but it seemed too easy. She felt like she would be taking advantage of her.

"Well, it's been a pleasure," Ronda said as she stood.

"You're not leaving?" Miranda said.

"Yeah. I should get home. I have practice tomorrow morning."

"Oh. That bums me out."

"Well, maybe I'll see you again sometime, huh?"

"Yeah. Maybe. We could start our own trivia team."

"That might be fun," Ronda said.

Ronda left the club feeling depressed. Miranda would have been a slam dunk, but it was too easy. She would have felt bad taking her home. She had seemed so naïve. Ronda questioned what exactly she was looking for. She just wanted someone to share her bed once in a while. And Miranda would have immediately tried to make them a couple. Ronda couldn't have that. Miranda would have been too easy to hurt. That was the bottom line.

She drove home and crawled into bed. She accepted that this was how things would be until the season was over. She was glad the season was starting soon to take her mind off her predicament.

Friday night rolled around and she dressed for the political fundraiser. Politics. Ugh. Gayla came over early and went over key points of the candidate's campaign.

"I'll just keep reiterating her stance on gay rights," Ronda said.

"I think just having you there does that. Focus on her other issues."

"Will do. If I can remember any of them."

"Better infrastructure. Increased jobs. Come on. How hard is this?"

"Okay. Okay. I can remember those."

"Good. Now, we should probably get going."

Ronda called a car and they went to a venue across town. The parking lot was full.

"This looks promising," Gayla said.

"Yeah. For you."

"For us. Now, come on."

They got out of the car and climbed the stairs to the Venetian style building.

"This place is impressive," Gayla whispered.

"I feel like I'm in Vegas."

"I know, right? Let's get inside."

They walked in to a high-ceilinged foyer. A woman greeted them there.

"Hello. I'm Ms. Shea. I'm Ms. Redman's campaign manager."

"It's wonderful to meet you," Gayla said. "I'm Gayla Adkins and this, of course, is Ronda Meyers."

"Thank you so much for coming. And Ms. Redman will be thrilled to meet you. She's a huge fan."

"Thank you," Ronda said.

"Drinks and hors d'oeuvres are along the back wall. Help yourself."

"Thank you," Gayla said. She took Ronda's arm and allowed herself to be led straight back to the table with the drinks.

They grabbed two glasses of champagne.

"Did you want something to eat?" Ronda said.

"How could I shake people's hands if I had a plate in one hand and a glass in the other?"

"I know. You keep telling me that. But I figured one of these days you might be hungry."

"Baby, eating every time I'm hungry isn't going to keep this figure of mine."

Ronda looked over her figure appreciatively.

"I'm sorry to hear that, but I do appreciate the sacrifice."

Gayla playfully slapped Ronda on the arm.

"Okay, you cad. Let's mingle."

Gayla led the way as they cut through the crowd. She greeted everyone they met with a smile and a kiss on the cheek. She introduced Ronda to everyone important.

"Can we slip outside for some fresh air?" Ronda finally said.

"Sure. Let's go."

They stepped out onto a patio where there were only a few people. The strings of white lights hung low and kept the party atmosphere.

"You doing okay?" Gayla said.

"Yeah. I'm just so darned tired of smiling."

"Aw, come on. With that winning smile? I'd have thought you liked to flash that any chance you got."

"Funny. I'm serious. My cheeks are getting sore."

"Okay, well, we're out here so you don't have to smile at the moment."

"Thank God. I suppose you're having the time of your life, huh?"

"Oh, you know it. Can you believe we met a real NBA player? And the fact that all these people have similar views to ours. It's awesome, isn't it?"

"I'm not as easily impressed, I guess."

"Why? These are big name people. And they're all for gay rights." Gayla brought up Ronda's key issue.

"Or so they say. Then we elect them and what happens? Where are our rights?"

"Oh, ye of little faith," Gayla said. "Come on. You've got to believe. We have to. Or where does that leave us? A couple of cynics never daring to hope? You're bigger than that."

"Or am I?"

"You are. What's with you? You seem out of sorts. You have all week. Does this have anything to do with Sunday?"

"No. Not at all. I'm fine."

It was partially true. It had nothing to do with Sunday. It had everything to do with only having Gayla for a playmate. She worried she'd get bored with her or hurt her or do something stupid in some way that their relationship would change. And she didn't want that to happen. She wanted their relationship to stay the same.

"Okay. If you say so. But maybe we should cut the extracurricular activities for a while."

"Why? Is that really what you want?"

"No. But I think it's what you want. Though I don't know why. I don't feel like I put any demands on you."

"You don't. Believe me. I don't want to change a thing about us."

"Are you absolutely positive?"

"I am. I also don't want to harsh your buzz, so let's get back in there and press some more flesh."

She offered her elbow which Gayla took and they went back to the party. Ronda felt better having talked things out with Gayla. The last thing she wanted was to lose her last playmate.

Chapter Ten

That night, after the fundraiser, Ronda suggested they swing by Gayla's place to get her some clothes for the next day and night and she could just stay with Ronda that night. Gayla looked like she would object, but then agreed.

"If you're sure that's what you want."

"I'm sure."

They finally arrived at Ronda's house.

"I'm tired," Gayla said. "Would you mind if we just sleep tonight?"

Ronda didn't understand what was going on inside of her. She was horny as hell yet the idea of just sleeping seemed fine with her.

"Sure. That would be cool."

"What is up with you?" Gayla said. "You never used to say okay to just sleeping."

"I'm tired. That's all."

Though she didn't really believe that.

They slept until nine the next morning. Then Ronda stretched, rolled over, and ran her hand the length of Gayla's body.

"Wake up, sleepyhead. Time to rise and shine."

"You can start without me," Gayla mumbled.

"Ah. But that's not as much fun. Come on, baby. Open those emerald eyes and let me see the desire I know is in them."

Gayla opened her eyes and smiled at Ronda.

"You're so cute when you're horny."

"And I'm way horny, so I must be adorable right now."

Gayla laughed at her.

"Yes, baby. You're adorable."

Ronda rolled on top of her and nuzzled her neck.

"Damn, babe. You smell so good. I can still get a whiff of the perfume you had on last night. It's new, isn't it? I love it."

"Excellent nose, my dear. It is a new fragrance. I'm glad you like it."

"Mm. Yes. Makes me want to devour you."

"Help yourself," Gayla said.

Ronda nibbled a nipple then sucked it into her mouth as deeply as she could take it. She ran her tongue over it before releasing it to kiss farther down her body. She came to where her legs met and kissed up one inner thigh and down the other. Finally, she rested her cheek against one inner thigh before she licked Gayla from one end to the other. She licked and sucked and flicked, and soon Gayla was begging for release.

Ronda slid her fingers inside her while she sucked on her clit and Gayla pressed her face into her and gyrated her hips until she froze and cried out as she climaxed.

"Good morning to me," Gayla said.

"Mm-hm. Good morning to you. What a way to wake up, huh?"

"I could wake up like that every morning."

"Wouldn't that be nice?"

Ronda rolled over to her back and lay there, catching her breath.

"So now it's your turn," Gayla said. "Are you ready to be wide-awake?"

"You know it."

"Good."

She suckled one of Ronda's nipples and played with the other breast before moving her hand down Ronda's tight abdomen. She brought her hand to lie between her legs. She lightly stroked her before plunging her fingers deep inside.

Ronda arched off the bed to take every thrust. Gayla kept at it until Ronda screamed, a low guttural scream, as she came.

"Come on. I'm starvin'. Let's go get a bite."

"I can't spend this much time with you. I'll gain a million pounds."

"You don't need to worry about it, babe."

"I do. I look like I don't because I count damned near every calorie that enters my mouth."

"Whatever. Relax. Take a day off. Let's go get Mexican. I'm jonesin' for some carnitas."

"Oh, God. I'm not going to win this, am I?"

"Not a chance. Let's hit the shower."

They stepped into the dual head shower and washed away the morning's activities and started some new ones. Ronda scrubbed Gayla, then rubbed between her legs with soapy fingers. She was so slick it was fun to run her fingers over her. Gayla leaned against one wall as she reached her orgasm.

"You just don't stop," Gayla said. "I mean, I might not be able to walk for the event tonight."

"Oh. I'm sure you'll be fine."

"I don't know."

"Come on. Get dressed. I'm gonna die if I don't eat soon."

They drove to a small hole-in-the-wall restaurant and parked in back.

"You ready for some great food?"

"Are you sure we won't get food poisoning here?" Gayla looked around.

"I'm sure. This place is the best."

They sat out on the patio that faced a busy street. They were waiting for their food when a car full of people drove by.

"Meyers!" they called out. "We love you!"

Ronda waved to them. She smiled.

"Sometimes Houston can feel like a small town."

"Sometimes. Not often."

"I think it does. I bet if I lived in other cities people wouldn't recognize me on the street."

"You're crazy. People in other cities would recognize you now. I can't imagine if you played for their home team."

"You really think so?"

"I do."

"I don't know."

The waiter brought their food, as well as a beer for Ronda and an iced tea for Gayla.

"I can't believe you got a flippin' salad. All this good food and you got a salad."

"I don't exercise like you do, Ronda. I mean, sure, I work out, but nowhere near to the extent you do. The calories don't slip right off me like they do you."

"Fair enough. You just always look so good."

"So do you. But even you admit, you work hard for it."

"Yeah, I do."

They finished their lunch in silence.

"So, what should we do today?" Ronda said.

"I have no idea."

"I'm thinkin' the zoo. Or the beach."

"Oh, let's go to the beach. I know we won't have much time there, but I'd love to go see the water."

They set off and in forty-five minutes were in Galveston. They rolled down their windows and let the fresh salt air wash over them.

"Oh, yeah. That's what I'm talkin' about," Ronda said.

"It's wonderful, isn't it?"

They stopped at a beachfront store and bought some beach chairs and sunscreen and set themselves up just at the water's edge. They waded out in the water until the bottoms of their shorts were wet, then they walked back to their chairs.

"This is awesome," Gayla said. "I love the beach and yet I always forget how close it is."

"Well, no more forgetting. We're going to come here a lot more after the season ends. It'll be hot here. We'll rent a room for a week."

"That sounds like fun," Gayla said.

"But what?"

"Huh?"

"It sounded like there was a 'but' in there."

"Nope," Gayla said. "No 'but' at all. It sounds wonderful. I just hope we actually remember to do it."

"We will. We have to. It's too invigorating not to."

The afternoon grew late and soon it was time to go. They threw the chairs in the back of the truck and headed back to town. Once there, it was time to shower and get ready for the night's event.

"Okay, you," Gayla said. "I'm going to shower first. Then you shower."

"You take all the fun out of it."

"We don't have time for fun. Save it for afterward."

"Ugh," Ronda said, but lay on the bed and waited her turn patiently.

They moved fluidly around each other as they dressed.

"I thought we'd be tripping all over each other getting ready," Ronda said.

"Are you kidding? Your bathroom is huge. There's plenty of room for both of us here."

"I guess that's a good thing."

"Sure it is. Who wouldn't want all this room to put your face on?"

"Oh, yeah. For putting my face on," Ronda said.

"Okay, well, for those of us who wear makeup, it's a treat to have such a large area."

Ronda checked out her double sink area and wondered what the heck all the bottles and tubes were that were neatly lined up. She knew Gayla went to a lot of trouble to look good, but jeez. She couldn't have guessed what all the products were.

But she was glad Gayla used them. She appreciated all the hard work Gayla did to keep up her appearances. Even though Ronda thought she was beautiful without all her face paint on.

She called for a car while Gayla put on her finishing touches. Ronda put her phone in her pocket.

"Why do you wear all this stuff?" she said.

"So you'll be proud to have me on your arm at these events."

Ronda thought she'd be proud to have her on her arm anywhere, but decided not to tell her. Somehow, the thought scared her.

"So, you ready to leave?" Ronda asked.

"Sure thing. Let's go."

They were relaxing in the car. Ronda had her arm around Gayla.

"So let me get this straight. We're going to help a bunch of rich doctors raise more money tonight. Is that right?"

"Baby, the doctors have money, but we're raising more for research and state-of-the-art equipment and whatever the doctors need to do their jobs. We're not raising money for the doctors."

"Well, why don't the doctors just fork over some of their money for the cause?"

"We're hoping they will. That's what the fundraiser's for. Oh, sure, there'll be the usual list of socialites there, but there will be a lot of doctors there and we plan to dig deep into their pockets."

"Doctors bore me."

"I'm sorry to hear that. But, if, God forbid, you got injured in a game, I'd like to think the equipment they used to test and treat you with would be top-of-the-line."

"Well, I guess when you put it that way…"

"Yeah. You guess."

They arrived at the event and Ronda took a deep breath.

"All right. Let's do this."

This fundraiser seemed to have potential, what with the live band set up at one end of the room.

"Wow. There's gonna be dancing?" Ronda said.

"It looks like it."

"Will you dance with me?"

"Right now?"

"No. Not right now. Later. When things get going."

"Sure, I'll dance with you."

The idea made Ronda smile. She reached across her body and patted Gayla's hand. They cut through the crowd to get some champagne and Ronda filled a plate with appetizers. They made their way to a table where they sat down so Ronda could eat before mingling.

"I'm starving," Ronda said. "We should have eaten before we came."

"You'll be fine. We'll get dinner after."

"Nothing will be open."

"Sure they will. We'll find somewhere."

Ronda finished her plate and stood.

"Okay," she said. "Let's do this."

"Great." Gayla affixed her wonderful smile on her lips and Ronda wanted to kiss her in the worst sort of way. She supposed she could have, being that her sexuality was public knowledge. She just felt funny kissing Gayla in public. So she didn't.

They visited with several doctors and their wives as they circulated through the crowd. They were constantly stopped as people wanted to meet Ronda Meyers and talk football. She actually found herself enjoying the event. She was concerned that Gayla might be feeling overshadowed, though.

"How you doin', babe?" she asked her.

"I'm doing great. How are you?"

"I'm actually having fun."

"Oh, good. I'm happy to hear that."

"Shall we dance for a while?" Ronda said.

"Are you sure you want to?"

"I love dancing."

"Okay, then let's go."

They grooved to several songs from the eighties. Ronda was pleased to see Gayla was such a skilled dancer. She loved to watch her move with the rhythm. It had Ronda thinking of other rhythms they'd be moving to later that night.

The band slowed the tempo and Ronda moved to take Gayla in her arms.

"I think we should sit this one out. Besides, I'd like some more champagne," Gayla said.

"Sure." Ronda fought to hide her disappointment. She escorted Gayla back to the champagne table. They each got another glass and sought a place to sit. They found an empty table and were relaxing when several doctors walked up and started talking football.

Ronda sat up straighter and engaged with them. They had some questions about some of the players who had been traded and who was still on the team. Some had questions about investing in the team. Gayla fielded those questions. She was more informed on that subject.

The doctors excused themselves and Ronda leaned back in her chair.

"This has been a great night. Why can't more of these shindigs be like this?"

"I think they're all fun. I guess you just like it because more people than usual are asking you about football."

"Yeah. Who knew doctors could be so much fun?"

"You might want to lower your voice when you say that."

"Oh, yeah. Right."

They laughed. And looked around. No one seemed to have heard Ronda's declaration.

"I think you got away with one there," Gayla said.

"I know, right? I'd better be more careful. Now, you ready to dance some more?"

"Actually, I'm getting pretty tired. Would you mind if we called it a night?"

"You know you never have to ask me twice."

"You were wonderful tonight," Ronda said when they were in the car. "I don't know how that society stuff comes so natural to you."

"Yes, you do. I was raised in that environment. Society is in my blood."

"I guess I forget that because you're such a normal person."

Gayla smiled.

"I think if you quit judging and tried getting to know more people in society, you'd find they're all normal people. Actually, I'd think you'd know that by now."

"I don't really take the time to get to know the people at the parties. I smile when appropriate, but that's about it."

"Well, maybe we should work on that."

"Yeah, maybe."

The car dropped them off at Ronda's house. Gayla sat on the porch while Ronda went inside and poured them a couple of drinks.

"I love your house," Gayla said when she returned.

"Thanks. It's home."

"It's so you."

"Yeah? How so?"

"Bigger than life."

"Is that how you see me?" Ronda said.

"I think that's how you see yourself."

"I'm just me," Ronda said.

"To me, you are. You let your façade down with me. And I'm not sure why."

Ronda was getting uncomfortable with the conversation. She was always herself. Except when she had to be Ronda Meyers, super football player, at those events Gayla dragged her to. Of course she was herself with Gayla. Why wouldn't she be? Whatever, she thought. She searched for a change of subject.

"So, you think we raised some money tonight for new medical equipment?"

"I do. I think it was a very successful fundraiser. Did you see what the bid was on your jersey in the silent auction?"

"No. I never looked at it."

"It was ten thousand the last time I looked."

"What the hell? For an autographed football jersey? It's a good thing that money was going to a good cause. Because that's a waste of money."

"No, baby. That's not a waste. It's wonderful."

Ronda was embarrassed that her jersey would go for that much. But Gayla was right. It wasn't a waste.

"You about ready to head to bed?" she asked.

"Sure." Gayla smiled at her.

Ronda held the door open for Gayla and admired her figure as she passed in front of her. She ran her hand down her back and over her shapely ass.

"You're beautiful." She pulled Gayla into her arms.

"You give me chills when you touch me like that."

"Is that a good thing?"

"Mm. Very."

"Then I should touch you like that more often."

Ronda brushed an imaginary strand of hair off Gayla's face. She traced her cheek with her thumb. She looked into her green eyes and got lost in them.

"Are you ever going to kiss me?" Gayla said.

"Mm. I was thinking about it."

Ronda lowered her mouth and claimed Gayla's. It was a soft kiss at first, but soon grew more passionate. Gayla opened her mouth and Ronda allowed her tongue to wander in. Ronda broke the kiss and leaned her forehead on Gayla's.

"Damn, woman. You sure can kiss."

"You're no slacker yourself," Gayla said.

"I need to get you in bed," Ronda said. "Like, right now."

"You won't hear me argue."

They continued to kiss as they fumbled their way down the hall until they came to Ronda's bedroom. They stripped each other's clothes off, and soon Ronda was holding a nude Gayla against her body.

"I love the feel of you against me," she said.

"It only gets me hotter," Gayla said. "Come on. It's time for you to take me."

She lay down on the bed and spread her legs. She dragged her fingers over herself.

"Are you just going to stand there? Or are you going to join me?"

"Oh, baby," Ronda lay down beside her. "I wasn't about to just stand there and let you have all the fun."

She kissed her again then rolled off her and reached in the drawer of her nightstand. She took out the doughnut toy.

"Do you think you can handle this?" she said.

"Oh, God yes. Please."

Ronda positioned herself between Gayla's legs so she could use the doughnut on her clit and slip the fingers from her other hand inside her. It wasn't easy, but she got it done, and she was rewarded when she felt Gayla close around her fingers. She eased her fingers out, but left the toy pressed against her and Gayla called her name again.

Ronda lowered her mouth to Gayla and licked up the remnants of her orgasms. She brought Gayla to two more that way.

"I can't take any more," Gayla whispered.

"What? Come on."

"No. No more. Please."

"Okay, babe. No more."

Ronda moved up and took Gayla in her arms.

"That was wonderful, baby. I love your toys."

"They are fun, aren't they?"

"Maybe tomorrow I'll use one on you."

"Tomorrow, huh?" Ronda needed release right then.

"Yeah," Gayla said sleepily.

Ronda decided she could wait until morning, so she pulled Gayla to her and held her as they slept.

CHAPTER ELEVEN

Ronda awoke the next morning, aroused almost to the point of orgasm. When she woke up a little more, she realized Gayla was sucking on a nipple and using the doughnut between her legs. Before she could even say good morning, Ronda grasped the sheets tightly and cried out as the orgasms cascaded over her.

"Damn, woman. Thank you," Ronda said.

"You're most welcome. I figured I owed you that after falling asleep on you last night."

"That's okay. You were tired."

"I was fine until you wore me out."

"Well, you needed that."

"True. I did. And you needed to be woken up this way."

"Mm. But now I want you."

She rolled over so she was on her side and suckled one of Gayla's nipples while her hand sought the moist heat between her legs.

"You feel so good," Ronda said. "Open up for me, babe. Let me have you."

Gayla spread her legs and Ronda plunged her fingers deep inside her.

"You like that?"

"Oh, yes," Gayla said, "Oh, God, yes. That feels so good."

Ronda slid her fingers over Gayla's swollen clit and Gayla dug her fingernails into her back. She cried out Ronda's name as she came.

Ronda wrapped her arms around Gayla and held her. She fit so well in her arms. It never ceased to amaze her how perfect they were for one another.

"I think I'd like some breakfast," Gayla said.

"Excellent. We'll shower and go get something."

"Do you ever eat at home?"

"If I have to. I'd rather not, though. I do most of the time. Just not on weekends."

"And I'm only here on weekends," Gayla said.

"Yeah. I guess you are. Now let's go shower."

They showered and, as expected, Ronda took Gayla to several more orgasms.

"You're dangerous. One of these days I'm going to drown in that shower," Gayla said.

"Nah. I'd never let that happen."

They dried off, dressed, and climbed in the truck.

"Where to?" Ronda said.

"I want seafood."

"I know a great place where the brunch includes crab legs."

"Let's go."

They paid and sat down. Ronda ordered champagne for both of them.

"Should you be drinking? You're driving," Gayla said.

"I'll only have a couple. Don't worry. I'm also drinking coffee."

They went through the food line and both sat down with plates piled high.

"So, I have to ask," Gayla said. "What is this we're doing?"

"What do you mean?" Ronda's stomach clenched. She had a feeling this was going to lead to a conversation she didn't want to have.

"You know exactly what I mean, Ronda. Don't get me wrong. I enjoy it. I just want to know what it is. How I'm supposed to be feeling. What I'm supposed to be expecting."

"I don't know what you're talking about. Honest."

"Us, Ronda. What are 'we'?"

"What do you mean?" she asked again. "We're 'us.' Same as always."

"I don't know if it's same as always. We're spending a lot more time together. And we're sleeping together way more often." She lowered her voice for the last sentence.

"What's wrong with that?"

"Nothing. I just want to know what's going on in your head."

Ronda tried not to panic. She didn't want to have this conversation. What did it mean? She'd forced herself not to think about it and didn't want to start at that moment.

"Can we finish brunch and then talk about it?" She hoped Gayla would forget by the time they got home.

"Sure. But we're going to have this discussion," Gayla said. "So don't think you're off the hook."

Ronda tried to relax, but couldn't. Still, she enjoyed the food. She was a big eater. She burned off a lot of calories in her line of work, so it was okay to eat a lot. She occasionally worried about what would happen when she retired, but then put those thoughts out of her head. Retirement was still a few years off, she hoped.

They finished their food and Ronda leaned back in her chair. She patted her stomach.

"Oh, my God. I'm so full."

"I know. That was so good."

"I think I could use a nap."

"Yes. That sounds wonderful."

"Great. Let's go home."

Ronda told herself it wasn't important that she casually referred to her place as home. And she didn't consider asking Gayla if she wanted to be dropped off. That was no biggie, either. There'd be time to take her back to her place later.

They took a brief nap at Ronda's house. They both woke at the same time.

"So, what now?" Gayla said.

"I want to play in the pool."

"Okay. That would be great."

They went outside and jumped in the pool. They splashed around and swam laps and just enjoyed the warmth of the day. Ronda climbed out and lay on a lounge chair. Gayla soon joined her.

They lay in silence for a while before Gayla broke it.

"So, you're going to hate me, but I'm going to bring up that subject again."

"Which subject?" Ronda hoped it wasn't the one from brunch. Ronda saw nothing wrong with their relationship and didn't see how talking about it could make it better.

"You know which subject. I just want to know what we're doing. That's all."

Ronda thought hard on the question. What were they doing? Hanging out. Having sex. Going to fundraisers. Did it matter that Gayla was the only woman she was sleeping with? That wasn't intentional. Or was it? Had she really tried to meet other women? There had been Miranda, but she couldn't break that girl's heart. Had that really been why? Or had she felt guilty about Gayla?

She really tried to keep herself too busy to worry about emotions and relationships and the like. But could she remain faithful to Gayla if they decided to become a couple? The thought caught her completely by surprise. Yes. She was contemplating dating Gayla exclusively on purpose. Her body was covered in chills.

"Are you okay?" Gayla said.

"I'm fine. Just trying to come up with an answer for you."

"It shouldn't be that hard."

"Well, it is. See, in some ways, we're doing the same thing we've always done."

"And by that, you mean working together, going to events together, and sleeping together," Gayla said.

"Exactly."

"But this business of spending days on end together is new."

"Yes, it is. And there's something else that's new."

"What's that?"

"You're the only one I'm sleeping with right now."

"Is that by choice?" Gayla asked.

"I don't know."

Gayla nodded slowly.

"So, no wonder you don't want to have this conversation."

"Yeah. I mean, maybe we're in a relationship."

"Maybe we are."

"Would you be okay with that?" Ronda asked.

"I would. Would you?"

"I don't know. I've got so much going on in my life. I don't really have time for a relationship."

"And yet, I'm at everything you've got going. Including practices once in a while. And you know I'll be there for games. So, if you were going to be in a relationship with someone, it would make sense that it would be me, right?"

"I guess so. So, I guess we're already in a relationship, aren't we?" Ronda said.

"We are. But you need to decide if there are any feelings for me inside you."

"Do you have feelings for me?"

Gayla was silent for a few moments.

"I've always had feelings for you, Ronda."

Ronda was stunned. She hadn't expected that answer. She didn't know what she had expected, but that wasn't it. So now she had to ask herself how she felt about Gayla. She thought Gayla was wonderful. She loved to have her around. Her house always felt empty after she was gone. But she knew she had to dig deeper. She'd never questioned anything like this. Gayla had always been there for her. And she'd assumed she always would.

But how did she *feel*?

She was always excited at the prospect of seeing her. She thought she was gorgeous and she always missed her when she wasn't around. Maybe she really did have feelings for her. Maybe this was what it was supposed to be, after all.

She reached out her hand. Gayla put hers in it.

"I have feelings for you, too, Gayla. Let's not play games. Let's just consider ourselves an item."

"Not the most romantic declaration, but I'll take it." Gayla laughed.

"Sorry. I'm not used to this kind of thing."

"When was the last time you were in a monogamous relationship?"

"Wow. A long time ago. I was seventeen, in high school."

"And you've been sworn off them ever since?"

"Not really ever since. I told you. I'm terrified of getting traded. What happens then?"

"Well, with me, you don't need to worry about that because I work for you," Gayla said.

"That's true. Hey. This relationship thing could work out."

"Way to be so positive." She laughed.

Ronda laughed, too.

"You're so easy to be with. No one else comes close."

"So, how did it end up that I'm the only woman you're sleeping with?" Gayla asked. "Or do I want to know?"

"Believe it or not, I went out trolling earlier this week."

"You did, huh? And?"

"And I found this girl who worshiped me. But it didn't feel right, so I left."

"I wonder why it didn't feel right," Gayla said.

"Maybe because I like you. I don't know."

"Answer me honestly, Ronda. Do you think you'll be able to stay faithful to me?"

"Yep. I honestly have no doubt. As a matter of fact, I feel a sense of overwhelming relief now."

"Really?"

"Really. And I have an overwhelming desire to make love to you now."

"Is that right?"

"Yeah. Now that we're all official and all."

Gayla laughed.

"You're so cute."

"I think you're beautiful. But I tell you that all the time."

"But I know now that you mean it."

"I've always meant it, Gayla. I just didn't know I had feelings that went along with my thoughts."

Ronda got up and reached her hand down to Gayla.

"So, what do you say? Shall we go celebrate our newfound coupleness?"

"Coupleness? Is that even a word?"

"It is now."

Gayla took her hand and stood. Ronda led her into her room and eased her onto the bed.

"You got a little pink out there today," Ronda said.

"I need to be more careful. I can't be getting sunburned."

"Why? A little color isn't a bad thing."

"Skin cancer is."

"Okay. Fair enough. We'll get some sunscreen to keep here."

"Thanks, baby."

They made love and fell asleep again. Gayla woke Ronda up by shaking her.

"Ronda. Ronda. Wake up."

"Huh? What? Oh. Yeah. What's up?" Ronda cleared her head and recognized Gayla needed her attention.

"You need to take me home. It's seven o'clock. I need to get home."

"Why?"

"What do you mean why?"

"I mean what's the hurry? Let's go get dinner and then I'll drop you off. Or you could stay here again. That would be nice."

She pulled Gayla on top of her and nuzzled her neck.

"You want me to spend the night again?" Gayla said.

"Sure. Why not?"

"I don't want you getting tired of me."

"I couldn't. I won't. But if you think that's too fast, then at least let me take you out to dinner before I take you home."

"I'm still full from breakfast."

"You can't possibly be. But come on. I'm famished."

They dressed and Ronda took them to her favorite Italian restaurant. After dinner, she took Gayla back to Gayla's place.

"You sure you don't want to come home with me?"

"I'm not sure of any such thing. But I think it would be better for me to be home tonight."

"Fair enough. Tomorrow, pack an overnight bag, though, so you can stay with me, okay?"

"Okay, baby. If that's what you want."

"It is. Big time."

"Okay. Well, I'll see you tomorrow then."

"Okay. Sleep well."

"I will."

"Good night."

Gayla climbed out of the car and Ronda watched her walk to her door. It filled her with pride that she was her woman. Gayla was all hers. Nobody else's. It made her smile. And kept her smiling the whole way home.

The next day, practice went extremely well. The team was firing on all cylinders. They looked great, both offense and defense. Ronda worked extra hard before practice lifting weights and during exercises. She felt great, rejuvenated, invigorated. She couldn't stop thinking about Gayla and how right things were. And how lucky she was and how she wasn't going to do anything to screw up what they had.

During the scrimmage, though, she focused on the plays, determined to make as many tackles and knock down as many balls as she could. As the premier cornerback in the league, she had a reputation to uphold.

As had become the norm, at halftime, Coach Hindley called her to the sidelines.

"You're through for the day," she said. "Good work out there. It's lookin' like another MVP season for you."

"I sure hope so," Ronda said. She went in and iced and showered, then dressed for showing houses. She was thinking about cutting back on her second job as she drove over to meet Gayla. But if she did, she'd have nothing to do in the off-season and she'd be bored stiff. The thoughts were competing in her mind when she pulled into the driveway of the first house she was showing.

She saw Gayla's car parked on the street and went inside to find her in the kitchen. She sidled up behind her and placed her hands on her hips.

"Hey, babe," she whispered in her ear.

Gayla turned around to face her.

"Hey yourself, stud."

"How's your day goin'?"

"Good. How was practice?"

"Fun. Lots of fun."

"How sore are you?" Gayla asked.

"Not too sore for later." Ronda kissed her.

"Good to hear. Now, focus on the details I'm going to go over with you."

Ronda listened as Gayla explained what the buyers were looking for and why this house was perfect for them. She ran over all the top selling points and told Ronda what parts to try to overlook.

"Why didn't you ever get your license?" Ronda asked her. "You could be doing what I'm doing and making a lot more money."

"I'm too lazy. Besides, you pay me very well to be your assistant."

"That's true."

"Okay. Here they come. I'll see you at the next house." She gave her a light kiss on the lips and left.

Ronda showed four houses that day. She was wiped out by the time the last one was over. She sold two of the houses, though, which was good.

"Two sales, not bad," Gayla said.

"Cha-ching."

"Shall we go out for drinks to celebrate?"

"We shall. Follow me."

Ronda drove to The V. She knew from the previous week that it would be dead, so she and Gayla could enjoy a few drinks without worrying about a loud, raucous environment. She parked her truck and waited for Gayla to get out of her car.

"Going lesbian tonight, are we?" Gayla smiled.

"I figured this way we could relax over a couple."

"Right. Without being judged. Good idea."

They stepped inside the dark club. It was almost empty. Gayla and Ronda chose to sit at the bar. The bartender served them their drinks.

"Hey, you're Ronda Meyers, aren't you?"

"Yes, I am."

"I'm a huge fan."

"Well, thank you."

"Would it be totally uncool to ask for your autograph?"

"Not at all. I'll be happy to give it to you."

The bartender looked around and could only come up with a cocktail napkin. Ronda signed it for her. The bartender folded it neatly and put it in her pocket.

"How about one more just for the bar?" Ronda suggested.

"That would be awesome."

Ronda signed another one and the bartender taped it to the mirror behind the bar.

"That's fuckin' awesome," she said.

"Happy to oblige."

"It's kind of nice to sit here and enjoy a drink together without worrying about displays of affection," Gayla said.

"Yes, it is. I'm thinking this might become one of our go-to places."

"You used to come here to get your groove on, didn't you?"

"I sure did. And we still can. Later on. After the season. We can come here and move and groove together."

"You sure you wouldn't be tempted by all those other ladies shaking their stuff?"

"I told you, babe. I'm all yours. I promised I would be faithful and I will. There's no reason for you to worry."

She kissed her lightly and put her arm around her.

"It's just so hard to picture you going from a player to being with me."

"But," Ronda said, "I haven't really been a player in a while. It's been you and one or two others. Certainly not the different woman in my bed every night routine like it used to be."

"I'd like to know who the others were. Or would I?"

"No. You know I slept with Carleen once. I was planning on making her a regular, but then, as you know, I couldn't."

"And the other?"

"Not important. No one you know."

"Why aren't you still sleeping with her?" Gayla said.

"She's in a relationship now."

"Oh. So I'm like girlfriend by default."

"It's always been you, Gayla. I just never saw it. And now that I realize it, I'm the happiest woman in the world."

"I hope you'll always feel that way," Gayla said.

"I can't imagine that I ever won't. Now, you ready to head home?"

"Sounds wonderful to me."

Chapter Twelve

April eleventh finally arrived. It was the first game of the season. Ronda was pumped. She was so ready for this. She could smell in the air that it was football season. And their season opener was at home. Always a plus. There was a buzz in the air as she waited in the tunnel. They played at a local community college stadium and it was packed. There was magic in the air, and Ronda was ready to kick some ass.

Finally, the loudspeaker called out, "Ladies and gentlemen, your Houston Stars!"

Ronda led the team from the tunnel onto the field as the fans erupted. It was a heady feeling. One Ronda thought she'd never get used to. Ronda joined two other players in the center of the field for the coin toss. She called heads. It was heads. The Stars elected to kick off first.

With the ceremony over, the teams took the field for the opening kickoff. Ronda stood on the sidelines, chomping at the bit to get in there and play. The kick pinned their opponents on their own ten-yard line. It was time for the defense to do their thing. Ronda ran out onto the field, confident she'd be able to help her team. There were no butterflies or nerves. There was only excitement. She was ready for this moment.

The first play was a pass. Ronda watched the ball sail from the quarterback. She timed her jump perfectly and caught the pass just before the receiver did. She then cut through the offense until she made it to the end zone. Touchdown! What a way to start the game.

The crowd was going wild. Ronda could barely hear her teammates congratulating her. She ran off the field with the ball still in her grasp. She gave it to the equipment manager who knew to keep it for her. Her first pick of this season. And it had been an easy one.

Coach Hindley was at her side.

"What in the hell were they thinking, throwing to you right off the bat? Talk about overconfidence on their part."

"They were testing me," Ronda said. "Fail!"

"Well, good job, Meyers."

"Thank you."

Ronda ran back onto the field and took her position. The defense held them to three and out. There were two pass attempts and neither were thrown on Ronda's side of the field.

The offense was on the field and Ronda paced back and forth on the sidelines, stopping occasionally to praise one of her defensive teammates on a good job the previous series of downs.

The game went on in the Stars' favor. Their opponents never got their footing. The score was forty-two to seven going into the fourth quarter. The second-stringers were all in the game. Ronda was relaxing on the bench. She turned around and faced the stands. She easily picked Gayla out of the crowd. She was gorgeous in black slacks and a red shirt. The colors of the Stars.

Ronda headed across the field to shake hands with the other team when the game was over. She was talking with the other team's quarterback.

"I can't believe I threw that ball directly to you," the quarterback said.

"Rookie mistake. You'll get your feel for the game. You did pretty well today for your first game."

"We got our asses kicked."

"But you were solid. Don't doubt yourself. The team around you needs to step up, though."

"Thanks."

"No problem."

Ronda looked around her, but most of the team was heading for the showers, so she ran off the field. She soaked in ice before she showered. And when she walked out of the dressing room, there was Gayla waiting for her.

"You were amazing today." She kissed her.

"I picked my nose most of the day," Ronda said. "She quit throwing it my way."

"Yes, but that one interception was awesome."

"Thank you. That felt good."

"Is that the ball?" Gayla motioned to the ball Ronda had tucked into her elbow.

"Yep. First pick of the season."

"Right on."

"You want to come over?" Ronda said.

"Are you up for that?"

"Oh, yeah."

Gayla laughed.

"Well, then, I'd be a fool to say no."

"Let's go drop your car off at my place and then we'll go get something to eat."

"Seriously? Why not let me cook for you? I can stop by the grocery store if you don't have any food at home."

"I can grill steaks. I know I've done that before, but I have a couple more steaks I can grill and you can make the salads."

"Sounds wonderful."

Ronda got home and went inside while she waited for Gayla, who somehow had gotten left in the dust on the trip home. She slipped out of her dress clothes and put a robe on. She planned to hit the hot tub as soon as Gayla arrived.

Gayla arrived shortly thereafter and rang the doorbell.

"Babe," Ronda said. "You don't need to ring the bell. Not if you're following me home. Just let yourself in."

"Okay. You look very nice in just a robe."

"Yeah? There's one for you, too. I really want to relax in the hot tub. You know, to pretend I played a hard game out there."

"A hot tub sounds wonderful. Let me get out of these clothes."

"I'll meet you out there."

Ronda was relaxing in the warm water when Gayla came outside. She watched as she took her robe off and set it on a chair.

"Don't hurry," Ronda said.

"What?"

"I'm enjoying the view."

Gayla stopped and put her hands on her hips.

"You are, are you?"

"Yes, I am. Very much," Ronda said.

Gayla slowly descended into the water. She crossed the tub to sit next to Ronda.

"This feels really nice," she said.

"Yeah, it does. Now come closer."

She wrapped her arm around her and pulled her close.

"That feels right," she said. She kissed her ear and cheek before turning Gayla toward her to kiss her lips. "That feels even better."

"Do it again," Gayla said.

Ronda was happy to oblige. She kissed Gayla lazily at first, but then with all the passion she was feeling. She brought her hand up to knead Gayla's breast.

"Oh, yes," Gayla said. "That feels amazing."

Ronda slid her hand down Gayla's body until she found her warm center. She slipped her fingers inside and rubbed Gayla's magic spot. Gayla buried her face in Ronda's shoulder when she cried out.

"Oh, my God," she said. "You are a most wonderful lover."

"Your body is easy to love."

"I wish we'd brought the doughnut out here with us. I really want to use it on you right now."

"Let's go to bed and you can use the real thing."

"It's not as good as the toy."

"Babe, you're better than the toy because you're you. And your tongue works wonders on me."

She climbed out of the tub and offered a hand to Gayla who took it and joined Ronda on the concrete. They dried off quickly before Ronda led her into her room. She lay down on the bed and opened her legs for Gayla.

"I'm so ready for you, babe. Make love to me."

"I can't refuse an offer like that," Gayla said. She climbed between Ronda's legs and licked and sucked at all she found there. Ronda raised her hips off the bed to meet Gayla's actions. She gyrated and moved against her. Finally, she couldn't stand it any longer and she called out Gayla's name as the orgasm washed over her.

"Not to be totally unromantic," Ronda said, "but I'm starving. You about ready for some meat?"

"Sure. Why not? I'll go get my robe on and start making the salad."

"Oh, yeah. Our robes are outside. You could always make the salad in the nude. I wouldn't complain."

"I wouldn't feel right," Gayla said. She climbed over Ronda and got out of bed. Ronda observed her appreciatively as she walked out of the room and out to the patio.

Ronda got out of bed and went outside to get her robe as well. She put it on, fired up the grill, then padded into the kitchen to get the steaks. She kissed and nibbled the back of Gayla's neck as she made their salad.

Ronda seasoned the steaks and took them out to put them on the grill. She was outside with them when Gayla came out. She sat on Ronda's lap.

"Hey, gorgeous. Did you miss me?"

"You know I did," Ronda said. And she meant it. She was surprised at how much she missed Gayla when they weren't together.

"You're such a smooth talker," Gayla said.

"No. I mean it. I miss you when you're not with me. I always have. Other women were just to fill that void. But I don't have to worry about that anymore."

"No, you do not. You'd better not try to fill any void with anyone else."

"Don't worry. I won't."

"Good. Now, how are those steaks looking?"

"Perfect. Would you mind bringing out a plate for me to put them on?"

Gayla returned with two plates. Ronda put a steak on each and followed Gayla into the house. Gayla served up the salads and they ate.

"That steak was perfect," Gayla said.

"The salad was delicious, too."

"We're such a good team."

"That we are. I'm so crazy about you, Gayla."

"Careful," Gayla said. "You might say something you regret."

"No, I won't. I'm crazy about you. I don't regret telling you that."

"Okay. I'm crazy about you, too."

"Good. That makes me happy," Ronda said.

She got up and cleared the dishes.

"Oh, no, you don't," Gayla said. "You pour yourself a scotch and relax. I'll put these in the dishwasher."

"Are you sure?"

Gayla kissed Ronda.

"Of course I'm sure. Pour me a scotch, as well. This won't take long."

Ronda did as instructed and was sitting in the living room with her feet up watching television when Gayla came out and joined her.

"What are we watching?"

"I recorded the game. I thought I'd watch it."

"Okay, sounds good to me. I certainly enjoyed watching it the first time."

"I just want to see how they played overall and I want to see how we played. Did I miss anything out on the field?"

"I don't think so. They didn't throw anywhere near you after your interception, baby."

"I didn't think so, but I want to see for sure."

They turned the game on. Ronda wrapped her arm around Gayla, who rested her head on Ronda's shoulder. Ronda rubbed her hand up and down Gayla's arm and soon heard the soft snoring that indicated Gayla had fallen asleep. Ronda checked the clock. It was only ten thirty, but she figured if Gayla was tired, they could go to bed.

She gently shook her.

"Gayla?"

"Hm? Jesse?"

"Gayla, wake up, babe."

"Jesse?" She opened her eyes and looked at Ronda with confusion.

"Jesse?" Ronda said.

Gayla's focus cleared.

"My brother. I was dreaming about him."

"You sure?" Ronda said. "Jesse's also the other starting corner-back on the team. You sure you weren't dreaming about her?"

"No. It was my brother. I assure you."

Ronda didn't like what she was feeling. Jealousy wasn't her thing. She'd never cared enough about anybody to be jealous. But she was jealous of Gayla.

"Baby, why would I dream of Jesse Swanson? She's not even on my radar. My brother, on the other hand, is. He's always in trouble. And I just dreamed he robbed a car then crashed it. He was lying there on the side of the road not moving."

Gayla's eyes teared up.

"Sh. Sh," Ronda said. "It was just a dream."

Gayla buried her face in Ronda's chest.

"But it seemed so real."

Ronda felt her jealousy dissipate as her need to comfort Gayla took over.

"It's okay, babe. Let's go to bed and you'll go back to sleep and dream of more pleasant things."

Gayla nodded and let Ronda help her off the couch.

"It just seemed so real," Gayla said again.

"Yeah, but it was just a dream. Trust me."

"I'm going to call him. Just to make sure he's okay."

"Fair enough. Come on in the bedroom with me. You can call him from there."

She guided Gayla to the bedroom and sat next to her on the bed. She rubbed her back while she dialed her brother's number. There was no answer. She left a message.

"Are you going to be able to sleep?" Ronda asked.

"I think so. I've calmed down. And even though he didn't answer, that doesn't mean there's anything wrong with him. I think I can let it go and get some sleep."

"Okay."

They took off their robes and lay in bed together. Ronda wrapped herself around Gayla and held her close. They fell into a deep sleep. A sleep that lasted until Gayla's phone woke them at two thirty.

"Hello?" Gayla said with panic in her voice. "Why are you calling? What's wrong?"

She was silent and Ronda lay next to her. Rubbing her back.

"Oh, my God," Gayla said. "Where is he? I'll be right there."

"What?" Ronda said. "What's going on?"

"Jesse was in a car wreck."

"Oh, my God. That's creepy." Ronda wondered if Gayla might be psychic. How bizarre would that be?

"I need to go. I'm sorry."

"Oh, hell no. You're not going alone. I'm taking you. Where are we going?"

"They took him to Methodist."

"Okay. Get dressed and let's go."

Ronda drove as fast as she legally could and got them to Methodist fifteen minutes later. Gayla got out of the car and practically ran into the emergency room. Ronda followed at a distance and when she walked in she saw Gayla in the embrace of her parents' arms. She hung back and gave them their space. They finally split up and Gayla's father looked over and saw Ronda. Ronda's heart crawled into her throat. She hadn't considered how it would look, her driving Gayla to the hospital in the middle of the night.

He crossed over to her and she held her breath.

"Ronda. Good to see you." He extended his hand. "Thank you for being there for Gayla."

"No problem. How's Jesse doing?"

"He's in surgery. We were just about to go up to that floor. Come with us?"

"Sure." She walked over and took Gayla's hand. "Let's go."

They were seated in the surgical waiting room.

"So, what happened?" Gayla said.

"He drove his car into a tree," her mom said. "There were no passengers, so he only injured himself."

"Was he drunk?" Gayla said.

"They're running a tox screen," her father said. "Lord, I hope not."

"Me, too," Gayla said.

Ronda sat there quietly, not knowing what to say. Jesse had been in and out of trouble since she'd known Gayla. She'd met him a couple of times. He was nice enough, but always seemed to have a chip on his shoulder.

The doctor came out. Ronda and the Adkins stood.

"How is he?" her dad asked.

"Not good, I'm afraid. He made it through surgery, but it was touch-and-go. He had a lot of bleeding in his brain. He banged his head pretty hard. We reconstructed part of his skull. I can't guarantee he'll ever regain consciousness."

Gayla turned into Ronda's chest and cried. She sobbed loud and hard. Ronda could do nothing but hold her and rub her back. She felt so helpless. She said a silent prayer to the powers that be that Jesse would pull through.

"When can we see him?" Mrs. Adkins asked.

"It'll be a while. You might want to go get some sleep and come back in the morning."

"No way. We're waiting," Gayla said.

"Okay. Get comfortable. Someone will come get you when you can see him."

They sat down and Ronda kept vigil while one by one they all drifted off. She wanted to sleep, but wanted someone to be awake when they came out to get them. She kept herself awake freaking out over Gayla's dream earlier. How had she known Jesse would be in an accident? What else had she foreseen in her life? She wanted to have a conversation about it with her right then, but knew she'd have to wait. It was neither the time nor the place.

Finally, shortly after the sun came up, the doctor came through the doors again. Ronda woke everyone up.

"Hey, hey. The doctor's here."

The other three woke up and rubbed their eyes. They sat up straighter in their seats.

"Can we see him now?" Mr. Adkins asked.

The doctor looked from one to another of them.

"I'm sorry," he finally said. "Jesse didn't make it."

"What?" Gayla said. "There must be some mistake. You're thinking of a different patient. Jesse Adkins. Go check on him."

Ronda pulled her close, but she pushed away.

"I'm sorry, ma'am," the doctor said.

"My baby boy," Mrs. Adkins cried.

"Can we see him?" Mr. Adkins asked.

"Certainly. You can go back there and say good-bye."

Ronda hung back in the waiting room. Gayla grabbed her hand.

"Please," she said. "Please come with me."

"Are you sure?" Ronda was just fine not seeing a dead body.

"I need you, baby."

"Okay, babe." Ronda steeled herself and took Gayla's hand and walked in with them.

"He looks so peaceful," Mrs. Adkins said. "Like he's just sleeping."

Ronda thought that was an odd thing to say. His face was mostly wrapped in gauze due to the surgeries they did on his head.

They stood there for a while. Ten, maybe fifteen minutes. Ronda had no way of knowing. Finally, Mr. Adkins suggested they leave.

"Come on. Let's get going. We've got a lot to do now."

He wrapped his arms around a sobbing Mrs. Adkins and guided her out of the hospital. Ronda did the same with Gayla. They stood in the sunlight in front of the building. Nothing felt right. People were coming and going as if it was any other day and yet Gayla's brother had just died. It was a surreal feeling.

"What now?" Ronda asked.

"You go on home. I need to be with my parents right now," Gayla said.

"Are you sure?"

"I'm positive. We have things to do. You can go home. Thank you for being with me last night."

"Of course, babe. I'll always be there for you."

"Thank you. I'll call you a little later."

"Okay. Take care." She kissed her cheek, got in her truck, and drove home.

Chapter Thirteen

Ronda slept for a few hours, then got up and showered. She made it to the film showing at the stadium with five minutes to spare.

"You look like shit," Coach Hindley said.

"Rough night."

"How rough? What bar did you close down?"

"No. Not like that. Gayla's brother died last night."

"Oh, no. He was young. What happened?"

"He wrapped his car around a tree. We spent the night at the hospital, but he didn't make it."

"Hey, I'm sorry, Meyers. I know you and Gayla are close."

"Yeah. Thanks."

She managed to stay awake while watching the films. She listened intently to what the coaches said they needed to work on. She even took notes. But boy, was she happy when it was over.

As soon as they were dismissed she walked to her truck. She texted Gayla.

"Hey. How you doin'? Is there anything I can do?"

Gayla texted her back.

"We're making funeral arrangements. Can I come over later?"

"Of course."

"Okay. I'll see you then."

Ronda was at a loss. She didn't know what she should do to help Gayla out at a time like this. She drove to a florist but didn't get out of her truck. There would be flowers enough at the funeral. She decided to just drive home and wait for Gayla. She was sure she'd need lots of comfort and support, and Ronda was just the person to give it to her.

Ronda got home and slipped out of her clothes. She put on some trunks and a T-shirt and dove into the pool to swim laps. She swam until she was exhausted. She felt invigorated, even as the exhaustion weighed down her limbs. She loved exercise of any kind.

She pulled herself out of the pool and was surprised to see Gayla sitting there.

"How long have you been here?" she said.

"Not long. I didn't want to disturb you."

"You should have." Ronda towel dried off. "I'd hug you, but I'd get you all wet."

"That's okay. I don't care."

Ronda pulled her close and stroked her back.

"I'm so sorry this happened, baby. So sorry."

"Thanks, Ronda. So am I."

Ronda felt her crying and held her until the sobs subsided.

"Here. Let's get you inside," Ronda said. They went into the living room and sat on the couch. "Babe, there's something I have to ask you."

"Sure. Shoot."

"Well, I can't stop thinking about your dream. Does that happen to you often?"

Gayla started crying again. Ronda wrapped her arms around her.

"No," Gayla said. "Nothing like that has ever happened to me before."

"Wow. What a trip."

"I know. It's a horrible feeling."

"I'm sure. But you know it wasn't your fault. You couldn't have changed anything."

"I know. But still…"

"No. There is no 'but still.' It wasn't your fault. You even tried to call him to see if he was okay. You did your best. You just happened to have a bad dream."

"That came true."

"Not totally. The car he was in was his, wasn't it?"

"Yes. So at least he hadn't stolen a car. But the gist of the dream came true, Ronda. That's scary."

"It could have been a coincidence. I wouldn't stress over it."

"But you've been waiting all this time to ask me about it."

"I just wondered. And the fact that it's never happened before means it was a coincidence. Nothing more. Now what can I get for you?"

"I think I'd really just like a nap. Would you mind if I go lie down?"

"Not at all. I'll hold you until you fall asleep."

They lay together on the bed. Ronda had her arms around Gayla. Ronda still felt so helpless. She couldn't get inside Gayla's head to see what she was feeling. She wanted to help with arrangements but knew that was a family's function. She just felt like she wasn't there enough for Gayla and didn't know how to make herself be there more.

When Gayla was asleep, Ronda slipped out of bed and went to the kitchen. She made dinner for them. While it was simmering on the stove, keeping warm, she went out on the back patio with a beer.

"Dinner smells amazing," Gayla said.

"You're awake already?" Ronda said.

"It's been about two hours. I'd say that's a decent nap."

"Are you sure? You didn't sleep much last night."

"I'm fine. So, what's for dinner? I'm actually somewhat hungry."

"Somewhat?"

"Yes. Please don't be offended if I don't eat much. But it sure smells good."

"Great. Well, let's go in and serve up."

Gayla was quiet during dinner and Ronda had no idea what to say to get the conversation started. Or if she even should. So she ate in silence hoping Gayla would finally break it. She did.

"So, we're going to cremate Jesse tomorrow. The funeral will be the next day."

"Okay. When do you need me to be where?"

"I'd love for you to be at the funeral."

"What time?"

"I told my parents I wanted it at three o'clock so I know you can be there."

"I will definitely be there. What else do you need from me?"

"I just need you to be you, baby. I'm going to really have to lean on you these next few days."

"I'm here for you. I'll even skip practice if need be."

"No. I wouldn't dream of that. Life is for the living, as they say. Life goes on is another one. We need to keep putting one foot in front of the other and living life to the best of our abilities."

"Those are excellent words to live by," Ronda said. "But it's not always that easy."

"I want you to go to your practices. I will be fine. Or maybe I'll even watch your practices. It's not like I have a lot else to do since you don't show houses during the season."

"Okay. That actually sounds nice. That way I'll be able to keep an eye on you."

"I'll get through this, baby. It won't be easy. Jesse was my only sibling. But I'll get through it and you'll help me."

"As long as you allow me to help you. That's important to me."

"I'm going to need you to. I don't delude myself into thinking I'm strong enough to go this road alone."

"Good. So, lean hard on me. I'll be there for you."

They finished dinner and Ronda did the dishes while Gayla sat out on the patio. Ronda joined her with two glasses of scotch. She handed one to Gayla, who leaned forward on her lounge chair and allowed Ronda to sit behind her. She leaned back into her. Ronda wrapped an arm around her waist and relaxed with her drink and her woman. Overall, life was good.

"Were you going to stay here again tonight?" Ronda said.

"I'd like that. I don't want to be alone."

"That's fine. I'd like to have you here."

"I can go home tomorrow and shower and pack a bag so I can stay the next few nights, if that's okay."

"That'll be great," Ronda said. And she meant it. She wanted Gayla with her. Her protective instincts were in full swing and she didn't want anything to happen to upset Gayla any more than she already was. And staying with her would mean she could keep an eye on her.

"You're really wonderful, Ronda."

"No. I'm just crazy about you so I worry about you and would do anything for you. That just makes me human, babe."

"Well, I think you're wonderful."

"Thank you. So are you."

"Thanks."

They sat in silence as the sun set and the stars came out.

"It's a beautiful night," Gayla said. "The first of many Jesse won't see."

She started crying and Ronda held her as closely as she could.

"Let it out, babe. I've got you."

"When will the crying stop?"

"When it does. Don't try to fight it, Gayla. Feel your feelings. Let your emotions flow. Besides, it hasn't even been twenty-four hours."

"I know. Still."

"Still nothing. Let it out."

"I must look a fright with red puffy eyes. I can't believe I'm letting you see me like this."

"And I can't believe you'd worry about that. If you think I'm that shallow, I can't imagine you'd be with me."

"True. I know you're not shallow. It's just…"

"I know. You're always put together perfectly. And I appreciate that. But your brother just died. It's okay to let yourself go."

Gayla turned until she was facing Ronda. She buried her face in her chest and sobbed. Ronda felt so sorry for her. She couldn't imagine what it would be like to lose a sibling. She came from a fairly large family, and they were all still alive.

"Sh. It's okay," she said. "Let it all out."

They sat like that for a long while until Gayla had cried herself out.

"I'm sorry I'm not better company," Gayla said. "Maybe I should just go home."

"Don't be ridiculous. I'm not letting you go anywhere. You need me right now. And I need you here so I know you're okay."

"You're the best, Ronda."

"That's sweet of you. I'm just looking out for you."

"Would you mind if we went to bed now? I'm feeling pretty wiped out."

"Sure. No problem."

They stripped out of their clothes and Ronda had to force herself not to crave Gayla's body. She needed to be held and that's what Ronda was there for.

The next morning, they had coffee together.

"Do you want me to be with you when he's cremated?" Ronda asked.

"No. I mean, thank you, but we decided to keep it family only."

"Okay. Well, I'm going to go to practice then. Here."

She handed Gayla a key to her house.

"In case you need a place to crash after. And if I'm not home yet, I want you to be able to get in."

"Ronda, are you sure?"

"I'm positive. I want you to come here. I want this to be your headquarters for the next few days. Okay?"

"Thank you so much." She threw her arms around Ronda and hugged her tight. "You're the best."

"No. I just care about you. That's all. Hey, I've got to get going. You going to be okay?"

"I'll be fine. Thanks."

"I'll see you this afternoon."

Ronda left for practice feeling uneasy about leaving Gayla home alone. But she was a big girl and Ronda did have responsibilities. She made it to the gym before anybody else and pushed herself hard, trying to forget the pain Gayla was experiencing. By the time it was time for scrimmages, she was almost exhausted.

"You okay?" Coach Hindley asked.

"Yeah. Why?"

"How's Gayla?"

"As good as can be expected."

"Hey, if you need time off..."

"No, like I said. I'm good. She's got her family. And the funeral tomorrow is after practice. So, I'm right where I need to be to keep myself busy and she's doing what she needs to do."

"Okay. If you're sure. But if your head's not in it, you could get hurt and I don't want that happening."

"Don't worry, Coach. My head's in it."

"Good. Now, go get 'em."

It was a good practice. Ronda got some good hits in and even made an interception. Canfield came up to her after her shower.

"Way to make me look bad out there, Meyers."

"Hey, I'm just doing my job. If you throw the ball to me, I'm going to catch it."

"You think you're so fuckin' awesome."

"Whoa. Slow down, Canfield. We're all on the same team."

"Yeah, but you have to make everybody else look bad. So uncool."

"No. I have a job to do. I'm supposed to do it well. And I practice the way I play in the games. Just like you. So, if you or any other QB throws one right to me, I'm going to catch it."

Canfield chest bumped Ronda.

"So you're saying I'm gonna throw a pick in the next game."

"Easy there, Canfield. I'm saying maybe be more careful."

"I'm gonna make you look so bad next practice."

"I wish you would. I'd rather you burn me and get a touchdown. But I'm not going to dumb down my position for you. If you want that TD, you're going to have to earn it."

Just then, Mallory walked up. She took Canfield by the arm.

"Come on. Let's go."

Canfield cast one more angry look Ronda's way before allowing herself to be led off.

"What was that about?" Coach Hindley was at Ronda's side.

"Ah, she was just pissed that I picked her today."

"It was a great play," Hindley said.

"Yeah, but she thinks I was trying to make her look bad."

"We're all on the same team," she said.

"I hear you."

Ronda left the practice center and headed for her house. She was hoping Gayla would already be there, but she wasn't. Ronda was tired from practice but keyed up with nervous energy. She dove into the pool and swam some laps. When she finished, Gayla still wasn't there.

She put on some shorts and a T-shirt and opened a beer. She settled in front of the television to see what was on. She heard a knock on the door. When she answered it, there stood Gayla, eyes red and puffy. She immediately took her in her arms.

"Oh, babe," she said.

"He's gone," Gayla said.

"I know, babe."

"No. He's really gone now."

Ronda was at a loss. She had no idea what to say, how to react. Gayla had just had her brother cremated. He had been turned into ashes. What do you say when someone's been through that?

"It's okay, Gayla. It's what he wanted."

"I know. But he was too young."

"Yeah. No doubt about that. Come on in. Sit down. Can I get you something to drink?"

"I'd love a scotch."

"Coming right up."

She poured the scotch, took a deep breath and brought it to Gayla. She handed her the drink then sat next to her on the couch.

"Do you want to talk about it?" she asked.

"What's to say? We went in there and waited until they brought him out to us in a box."

"A box?"

"Yes. It's a nice wooden box. I don't know."

She started bawling again. Ronda rubbed her back, at a complete loss for words.

"Can I get a tissue?" Gayla asked.

Ronda brought her a box.

"So, who will keep the box?" Ronda asked.

"He'll be inurned tomorrow after the service. Please tell me you'll go with me to the ceremony."

"Of course. I'm here for you, Gayla. Any way you need me."

The next day at practice, Ronda had to mentally tell herself to focus. She was worried about Gayla and the funeral and inurnment. She hadn't been to a funeral herself in her adult life. It wasn't going to be easy, but she had to be strong for Gayla. Practice finally ended and she headed home.

Gayla was there, in a black dress that normally Ronda would have commented on how lusciously form-fitting it was. But now was not the time or place. She looked at Gayla's face and noticed that even the makeup couldn't hide the splotchy patches and the red, swollen eyes.

"I can't believe this is happening," Gayla said as she stepped into Ronda's arms. "I can't believe we're essentially burying my little brother today."

"I'm here for you, babe. Lean on me. Come on in my room while I get dressed."

Ronda went through her closet and chose a black suit with a black shirt. She would be hot, but it was appropriate for a funeral.

"They want this to be a celebration of his life," Gayla said. "But he was always in trouble, so what's there really to celebrate?"

"He was a troubled kid, sure. But he was a good guy, too. I certainly enjoyed his company the few times I met him."

"Thanks, Ronda. That's sweet of you to say."

"I mean it." She checked herself out in the mirror. "Are you ready to go now?"

"No. I'll never be ready. But we have to. Let's do this."

Gayla laced her hand through Ronda's elbow and they walked out to the truck. Ronda held the door and Gayla climbed in. Ronda climbed in and drove to St. Paul's Methodist Church. The parking lot was full. She found a place to park and they climbed out. Ronda didn't know how much public display Gayla would be comfortable with, but Gayla held her hand and squeezed it. Ronda saw tears flowing down her cheeks.

"Do you want to take a moment?" Ronda asked.

"No. It won't matter."

"Okay."

They walked in and Gayla led Ronda to the front row with the rest of the family. Ronda felt like she stuck out like a sore thumb, but if that was where Gayla needed her to be, that was where she would be.

The ceremony was lovely. The preacher spoke kindly of Jesse, even though Ronda doubted he'd ever met him. Then it was Gayla's turn to talk. Ronda hadn't expected that. Gayla squeezed her hand then got up and made her way to the podium. Her speech was wonderfully poignant with only a few breaks to compose herself. She came back and sat down.

"You did good," Ronda whispered in her ear.

Gayla smiled at her through tears and squeezed her hand again. They held hands throughout the rest of the funeral and then followed Gayla's parents out to the limousine that was waiting to take them to the Memorial Garden which would be Jesse's final resting place.

Chapter Fourteen

The days after the funeral were hard for Gayla. She split her time between her parents and Ronda. Ronda always tried to be upbeat and positive for her, while giving her plenty of time and space to mourn.

Being there for Gayla during her tough time solidified Ronda's desire to be with her. She felt nauseous thinking about Gayla going through the death and inurnment of her brother all alone. Sure, she had family, but she'd needed more. And Ronda was proud to have been able to be more for her.

During that time, something had shifted in their relationship. It should have scared Ronda but it didn't. It should have sent her running for the mountains. Instead it sent her further into life with Gayla. And that was a good thing.

Ronda focused on her practices and was more than happy to have another game that weekend. It was a home game, too, which meant Gayla would for sure be there.

"I'll look for you in the stands?" Ronda said as she left the house that Saturday morning.

"I'll be there."

"Good. Thanks."

She kissed Gayla good-bye and went to the stadium.

The game was a close one. Their opponent was a much better team than the previous week's. In the fourth quarter, the Stars were only up by seven points. Ronda was getting edgy. She liked to blow out the other team. They'd run the ball at her a few times and she'd tackled the runners, no problem. But they hadn't thrown the ball at her. Smart for them, but it left her bored over there.

With only three minutes left, the opponents passed the ball on Ronda's side of the field. She tracked the ball and watched where the receiver was. No problem. She reached out and grabbed the ball. As she fell to the ground, the offensive player fell on her leg. She heard a loud pop. She rolled around on the ground in agonizing pain. But she held onto the ball.

The next thing she knew, the trainer was out on the field, asking her questions and assessing her knee.

"What happened?" the trainer asked.

"I don't know. I just remember hearing a loud popping noise and then pain. Oh, my God, the pain," Ronda said.

"Look at how swollen it is already. Can you straighten it out for me?"

Ronda tried, but was unsuccessful.

"How about bending it. Can you get it to ninety degrees?"

Once again, Ronda was unable to do as she was asked.

"What is it, Doc? What's wrong?"

"Well, we need to do some more tests, but I think you tore your ACL."

"Oh, shit."

"Yeah. If you did, you'll be out the rest of the season."

"That sucks. You got any good news, Doc?"

"That you're going to get a nice ride off the field on this little cart and we'll take you to get an MRI."

"Gee, swell."

They got her on the cart and she gave the crowd a thumbs-up as they drove off. Not that she felt much like thumbs-up. She felt like crap. She was in pain and she didn't want to miss the season. Maybe it wasn't a torn ACL. Maybe that was a misdiagnosis. That would be cool.

In the locker room, the trainer helped Ronda get out of her uniform and into her street clothes.

"Gayla," Ronda said.

"What?"

"Where's Gayla? She needs to come with me."

"Is she your girlfriend?"

"Yes."

"I've seen her around. I don't know where she is. Right now, we need to get you checked out. Now, how is your pain, on a scale of one to ten? Ten being highest."

"I don't know," Ronda said through gritted teeth. Nine?"

"Okay. Okay. Now, just hang in there."

They wheeled her out to the parking lot where the ambulance was waiting.

Gayla approached the group.

"Ronda? Are you okay?"

"Oh, thank God. There you are. Come with us?"

"I'll follow you in my car. What do they think is wrong?"

"They think it's a torn ACL."

"Oh, no."

"Yeah. Oh, no is right."

"Okay, you two. We need to get her to the hospital. You can talk more after the MRI."

They loaded Ronda into the ambulance and sped away. It arrived at the hospital where she was immediately put in a wheelchair and taken in for an MRI. She was helped into the tunnel and lay still as the machine whirred around her. When the MRI was over, they wheeled her out to a waiting room, where Gayla sat looking nervous. She rose and greeted them.

"How are you?" she asked.

"I'm in a lot of pain. They're gonna see about getting me some pain pills. Do you know how the game ended?"

"No. I left as soon as I saw you go down."

"Damn."

"I'm sure the coaches will be here as soon as they can to check on you and they'll tell you then. I can tell you your pick stood."

"I figured. I wasn't letting that ball go. Hey, did it look like the offensive player went for my knee?"

"What do you mean?" Gayla said.

"I mean, was it intentional?"

"Well, I didn't see any replays, but real time it looked like she just happened to land on you."

"Okay. That's okay, I guess."

The trainer was back in the waiting room.

"Did you find anything for the pain?" Ronda asked.

"No. If they're going to do surgery, they can't give you any meds until then."

"Holy fuck. This hurts, though."

"Hang in there, Meyers. You're a tough one."

"Surgery? Is that the way to go?" Gayla said. "And, if so, shouldn't you wait a few weeks? I thought that was protocol."

"Actually," the trainer said, "studies have shown that if you do surgery immediately, your body is only recovering from essentially one trauma rather than two. So, we're recommending surgery. But we want to talk to Coach Hindley before we make any decision."

"Well, she'd better get here soon or I'm going to pass out," Ronda said.

Gayla took her hand.

"Hang in there, baby."

Just then Coaches Hindley and Poehl came rushing in.

"How are you?" Hindley asked.

"I fucking hurt. Now can we decide whether or not I'm having surgery?"

"Sure," Poehl said. "Let us all talk and we'll come back. What's your take?"

"I vote for surgery."

"Fair enough. We'll keep that in mind."

The trainer, surgeon, and both coaches stepped off to the side and engaged in a quiet conversation. It seemed to last for hours. Finally, they broke it off and came over to Ronda.

"We're going to do the surgery," the surgeon said.

"Excellent. Now give me some drugs to knock me out."

"Soon, Ms. Meyers. I'll have a nurse take you up to pre-op where we'll get you ready."

"Fine." Ronda reached out and grabbed Gayla's hand.

"I'm not going anywhere," Gayla said. She stood back as the trainer wheeled Ronda and she and the coaches followed. They all packed into the elevator and rode it up to the surgery floor. The trainer was in charge. She checked in at the desk and then they all waited. Finally, Ronda got called back to a room. Everyone rose.

"I'm sorry," the nurse said. "Only one person may go with her."

Everyone looked at each other, but Ronda reached out and took Gayla's hand.

"Gayla will go with me."

The others nodded and sat down. Gayla followed the nurse as she wheeled Ronda into a room. The nurse left them alone with instructions for Ronda to strip out of her clothes and put the gown on, opening in the back.

"I'll be as gentle as I can getting your slacks off, but let's face it, it's gonna hurt," Gayla said.

"Yeah. Here. Let me get my jacket, shirt and bra off first."

They got them off and Gayla carefully folded them and put them in the bag she'd been given. Now it was time to get Ronda's slacks and underwear off.

"Maybe straighten both legs and I'll slide them off?" Gayla said.

Ronda did her best and lifted herself off the bed enough for Gayla to slide both her slacks and boxers down and off her.

"Oh, shit," Ronda said.

"What?"

"Nothing. I just fuckin' hurt."

"I get that, baby. It'll be over soon."

"No. That's just it. It's only just starting."

"Well, I suppose that's true. But the pain you're in at this moment will be gone soon."

There were nurses in and out asking questions and setting up IVs, as well and the anesthesiologist came in. Gayla felt like she was in the way, but knew Ronda wanted her there. Finally, the anesthesiologist gave Ronda something to calm her down and told Gayla they'd come get her after surgery. They wheeled Ronda down the hall, but that was all she remembered.

❖

Ronda awoke feeling stoned some time later. She shook her head to try to clear the cobwebs, but they persisted. She was happy to see Gayla standing there. She reached out for her.

"Babe, you're here."

"Of course I am. How are you?"

"I'm messed up. Whatever drugs they gave me were great." She laughed.

"Well, I suppose there are worse things to hear. How's your knee?"

"What knee?" Ronda laughed again. "I can't feel anything, so I'm okay now."

"Well, enjoy it now. It's going to hurt like a mother soon enough."

"Thanks, babe. You always know the right thing to say."

"Hey, baby, I need to get out of here. Coach Hindley and Coach Poehl are dying to get in here to see you. I'll be outside in the waiting room, okay?"

"Give me a kiss."

They kissed and Gayla left the room. Her coaches came in next. It was a crowded room, but they both apparently felt the need to check on their star.

"How you feeling?" Hindley asked.

"Stoned. How are you?"

Poehl laughed.

"Fair enough. How's the knee?"

"I can't feel it right now, which I'm guessing is a good thing."

"The doctor said everything went perfectly," Hindley said. "He said you should recover fully."

"Yeah, but when?"

"It's going to take time, but you should be one hundred percent. And then you'll be back to being a menace on the field."

"I sure hope so. I'd hate to think I'm never going to play again."

"Get that thought out of your head," Poehl said. "We're going to work with you to make sure you get the best treatment possible.

You'll have the team physical therapist at your house working with you. The surgeon was one of the best in the country. You're in good hands, Meyers. Trust us."

"Good."

A nurse came in and ushered the coaches out of the room.

"Who's taking you home?" she asked.

"Gayla Adkins."

"Is she in the waiting room?"

"Yes."

"I'll go get her."

"Am I leaving now?"

"Not right now. We have lots to go over with you. But she should be in here to hear what we say. You're going to be under the effects of anesthesia for about twenty-four hours, so we like to be sure we're giving instructions to someone coherent."

She left the room, but returned moments later with Gayla at her side. She handed Gayla the prescription for Ronda's pain medication and anti-inflammatories.

"Be sure to stop and get this filled on your way home," she said. "You need these. I want you to take these as ordered. Don't try to be a hero and go without them. You want to stay ahead of the pain. Once you get behind it, it's not fun playing catch-up."

Gayla nodded and looked at Ronda.

"Got it," Ronda said.

"Great. A therapist will be in soon to go over the use of crutches with you. I can't stress this enough. Use them. The first couple of days, your thigh may be numb. You're going to be sure to use crutches so you don't fall. You don't want to twist or otherwise injure your knee."

The nurse left and Gayla sat holding Ronda's hand.

"This is like my worst fucking nightmare," Ronda said. "A torn ACL. Shit."

"But you're going to get better and you're going to play again and you're going to rock that football field."

"But this season is over, right? No MVP for me. God, this is frustrating."

"I know, baby. It must be. I'm so sorry."

Ronda squeezed her hand.

"I guess it is what it is at this point, huh? I need to accept that it happened and work on getting better."

"That's exactly right," Gayla said. "And I'll be here every step of the way to help you."

"Thanks, babe."

They waited for what seemed an eternity, and finally, a physical therapist came in and showed Ronda some range of motion exercises to do at home. He also got her up on crutches and instructed her on how to use them.

"It seems to me crutches would be intuitive," Ronda said.

"But you're not going to have any feeling in your thigh the first couple of days. It's imperative you not try to bear any weight on that leg."

"That's what the nurse said, too," Gayla said. "We'll be careful."

"After a couple of days, you're encouraged to bear as much weight as you can. You can bend your knee, just not to ninety degrees. Be sure to elevate your leg for pain relief and to reduce swelling."

"That's a lot to remember," Ronda said.

"It's all in this paperwork I'm giving to your friend," the therapist said.

"Okay. Thank you," Ronda said.

"Have you thought about where you'll be doing your therapy?"

"At home. The therapist from the team will be doing my therapy."

"Oh, good," the therapist said. "Then you'll have access to the team's equipment as you progress."

"Exactly."

"You're lucky."

"I know," Ronda said.

The therapist left them alone.

"How are you feeling?" Gayla said.

"I'm doing okay. Less foggy every minute."

"Good. Now let's get you dressed."

It wasn't easy, but Gayla was gentle and Ronda was patient, and together they got her out of her robe and into her street clothes. The nurse came back in the room with Ronda's discharge papers. Gayla left to get her car and Ronda was wheeled out to the exit. Her coaches were with her.

"Hey, will you guys bring my truck back to my house? I left it at the stadium."

"No problem. We'll go get it right now."

"Oh, yeah. And did we win?"

"Yep. Your pick probably saved the game," Hindley said.

"Excellent."

Gayla pulled up then and they wheeled Ronda to the car. She tried to stand up using the crutches and following the instructions the therapist had given her, but still, she almost fell.

"Whoa there. Easy does it," Hindley said. "Here, let me help."

They got Ronda in the car and Gayla drove to the pharmacy to get her prescriptions filled. They had to drop them off and come back in fifteen minutes.

"That's perfect," Gayla said.

"Why?"

"You can't take them for another couple of hours. And this way we can get you settled at home and then I'll go out and get them."

That's what they did. Gayla got Ronda situated on the couch, then left. Ronda lay her head back and fell fast asleep. She awoke to Gayla and the smell of barbecue.

"What smells so good?" she asked.

"It's dinner. I figured you'd had a pretty lousy day so I'd spoil you for dinner."

"Well, I do appreciate that, but I'm going to have to start watching what I'm eating since I won't be working out or playing for a while."

"Fine. You can start that tomorrow. But tonight you're having brisket and ribs."

"Oh, yeah. Now you're talking."

"Are you hungry?"

"I'm famished."

"Great. So, let's get you into a sitting position and we'll figure out how to feed you."

"I can feed myself," Ronda said. "But I would appreciate some help sitting up."

Gayla worked with her and Ronda used her good leg as much as she could, and they finally got her into an upright position.

"This sucks," Ronda said.

"Anything in particular or just the whole situation?"

"The whole situation. I hate being an invalid."

"You won't be for long. You'll be back on your feet in no time. I honestly believe that."

"Thanks. What would I do without you?"

"Let's not worry about that now."

Gayla handed Ronda her plate then took her own plate and sat at the end of the couch and ate her dinner. After dinner, Gayla did the dishes while Ronda fell back asleep. She awoke again to Gayla's soft voice.

"Baby, baby? Do you want to go to bed?"

"Hm?" Ronda said. "What?"

"Are you ready to go to bed?"

"I think so. I'm pretty wiped out. Can I have any pills yet?"

"Yeah. Let me go get them for you."

She gave Ronda one anti-inflammatory and two pain pills. Ronda swallowed them with water then allowed Gayla to help her to her feet. Gayla handed her her crutches and followed close behind her to the bedroom. She stripped Ronda of her clothes.

"Did you want some pajamas?" Gayla asked.

"No. You know I sleep in the nude."

"I knew you did when I was here." She smiled.

"I do when you're not, too."

"Okay. Fine. You're set. Do you have an extra pillow I can slip under your leg to elevate it?"

"Yeah. In the closet."

They got her situated and Gayla climbed into bed and snuggled up against her.

"Do you need anything else?" Gayla asked.

"Just for you to be here when I wake up."

"You don't have to worry. I'm not going anywhere."

Chapter Fifteen

The next few days were painful for Ronda. She tried to stay ahead of the pain, but it didn't seem to work. The pain pills made her feel good, but didn't seem to take away the pain. She was in a foul mood, even if she tried to stay upbeat and pleasant for Gayla.

"Baby, you're hurting. I don't understand why the pain medication isn't working," Gayla said several days after surgery. "I wish there was something I could do."

"Just be here for me, babe. That's all I can ask. I appreciate all you're doing for me."

Gayla was busy canceling any appointments Ronda had set up and screened all phone calls coming in. She was acting more like a secretary than she ever had before. But she seemed fine with it. She was also monitoring Ronda's meds, making sure she took them as prescribed.

"I'm here for you. I'll always be here for you."

The next Saturday, Ronda was propped up on her couch still wishing the pain would lessen. Gayla turned on the game for them to watch.

"I hope this will take your mind off the pain," Gayla said.

"Me, too."

The game was a close one, tied at halftime.

"I should be out there. I can't believe I got hurt. What a stupid thing to do."

"It wasn't your fault, baby. It was an accident. Accidents happen. Especially in football."

Then the opposing quarterback threw the ball at Ronda's replacement. It was a completed pass that went for an additional twenty yards.

"She should have picked that," Ronda said. "I can't believe she let that happen."

She reached for the remote.

"You're not turning it off, are you?" Gayla said. "One bad play isn't worth missing the whole game for."

But after several more throws to Ronda's replacement, they both decided it was time to turn the game off and find something else to do.

"I'm going to do some exercises," Ronda said.

"I'll get dinner going."

Gayla had been there for the whole week. Ronda was so grateful to have her there. She didn't know what she would have done without her. She really liked Gayla. That was obvious since Gayla hadn't gotten on her nerves yet. She was surprised by this, but pleasantly so. But having her around so much and sleeping with her every night had Ronda's hormones starting to act up. She didn't know if she'd be able to make love to her, but she certainly wanted to try. She decided that night would be the night.

She did her exercises and grabbed her crutches. She determinedly made her way to the kitchen and moved in close to Gayla.

"That smells delicious," she said. She nuzzled her neck. "You smell good."

"Thanks. Dinner should be ready in about ten minutes. What do you want to do?"

"How about we make out?"

"That sounds great to me, but how would your leg take it?"

"Let me go pop some pain pills and I'm sure it'll be fine."

"You're not due for pain meds until after dinner," Gayla said.

"Don't be a stickler. So I take them a little early. What's the harm?"

She took the bottle off the kitchen counter.

"Besides," Gayla said as she took them back. "You're supposed to take them with food. You'll puke all over the place if you take them on an empty stomach. Now just be patient."

Ronda didn't want to be patient. She was so horny for Gayla. She didn't care about her knee right then. All she cared about was kissing and touching and making love with Gayla. She pressed Gayla against the refrigerator and kissed her. She kissed her tenderly at first, but then harder as her passion flared.

"It's been too long," she whispered in her ear. "I need you so bad."

"Do you think you'll be able to? Make love to me, I mean?"

"I don't know, but I'm damned sure willing to try."

"I worry it'll hurt you," Gayla said.

"I can stand the pain."

"No. I mean like reinjure you or do something to your knee."

"I'll be careful."

"Well, hold that thought for now. Dinner's ready."

They ate in silence. Ronda tried to focus on the flavor of the dish Gayla had prepared, but was only aware of her closeness. She didn't give a flying fuck about her knee. She was going to have Gayla that night.

After dinner, Gayla gave Ronda her pain pills and anti-inflammatories.

"You know. I'm coherent now. I can manage my pills by myself," Ronda said.

"But then why would I have to be here?"

"For me. Just to be here for me. I love having you around."

"Yeah? That's sweet of you to say."

"Well, it's true," Ronda said.

"But if you can get along by yourself, I really don't need to be here twenty-four seven."

"Maybe not, but so what? You might not need to be here, but that doesn't mean you shouldn't be here."

"Well, we'll talk about it more later."

"Right. For now, I'm taking you to bed."

"Baby, it might be too soon."

"I promise I'll be careful."

The pain pills were starting to kick in, making her feel nice and relaxed. If only they took the pain away from her knee. She just figured the pain would be a lot worse if she wasn't taking them. Still, she wished the pain would be gone.

"Come on," she said. "Let's go to the bedroom. Sorry I can't hold your hand or anything."

"Ronda, I'm seriously worried. I don't think we should do this."

"It's been a week. I promise not to bend my leg too far and to stop if it starts to hurt worse or anything. Now, go on. I'll follow you."

They made their way to the bedroom. Ronda was quite proficient on her crutches so was right behind Gayla the whole time. She pulled her to her and kissed her again.

"God I've missed this," she said.

"Me, too. Now let's get you off your feet."

"First, let me undress you."

Gayla moved close to Ronda so she could unbutton her blouse, but Ronda was fumbling with the buttons, as she had to hold on to her crutches at the same time.

"Here," Gayla said. "You sit down. I'll get undressed and then help you with your clothes."

Ronda sat on the bed and watched with pleasure as Gayla undressed for her. She went nice and slow, just the way Ronda liked to be teased.

"You're killing me," Ronda said.

"But you love it."

"You know I do."

When Gayla was completely naked she stood in front of Ronda and got her undressed. They got her on the bed and Gayla put her crutches close to the bed so Ronda could get to them when she needed them. She climbed up on the bed next to Ronda.

"You sure about this?" Gayla said.

"I am. I've never been more sure about anything."

Ronda rolled gingerly onto her left side, careful not to put too much pressure on her knee.

"My God, you're beautiful," Ronda said.

"And you're hurting."

"I swear, I'm not." She was telling the truth. She'd found a position that was pain free, and she wasn't about to shift now that she was in it. "Just don't make me move, please."

"You're in charge, baby. I won't make you do anything."

"Okay. Great." She kissed Gayla then, a hard, passionate kiss that made her toes curl. She pressed her upper body into Gayla, feeling their breasts against each other. "Oh, yeah. That's it."

Gayla opened her mouth and Ronda slipped her tongue inside. She tangoed her tongue with Gayla's until she was so dizzy with need she thought she might pass out. Ronda skimmed her hand over Gayla's body. She pulled her breast to her mouth. She sucked and licked her nipple until Gayla mewled as she came. Ronda continued to suckle as she moved her hand down between Gayla's legs. She found her wet and ready for her. It had been so long. It felt good to feel the moist satin area that was Gayla.

"You feel so good," Ronda said. "I love how wet you are."

"That's all you, baby. All you."

"Mm. Well, I'm happy to help."

She slid her fingers inside Gayla and stroked her. She wasn't at it long when Gayla clamped down on Ronda's fingers and cried out as she reached her orgasm. Ronda guided her hand to Gayla's clit. It was hard and slick.

"God, I wish I could taste you," Ronda said.

"So do I."

Ronda pressed her clit into her pubis and Gayla came a third time. Ronda opened the table on the nightstand. She pulled out their doughnut toy and turned it on. She pressed it into Gayla.

"Oh, God," Gayla said. "Oh, yeah. That feels so good."

"Yeah? Is this what you needed?"

"It sure feels amazing," Gayla said. "But I'd rather feel your tongue."

"I don't know if I'm as talented as this thing."

Gayla started to respond.

"Sh. Don't think about it. Just enjoy it. Let it go. Feel the magical tongues working on you."

"Oh, God," Gayla said. "Oh, Jesus, Ronda. I'm gonna come. Oh, God. Yes."

She arched her back and gripped the sheet under her. Ronda kept at it until Gayla grabbed her wrist.

"No more, baby. I'm too sensitive now."

"Fair enough," Ronda said. She was feeling sleepy by then. She rolled over to her back and pulled Gayla against her. They fell asleep.

On Monday, the physical therapist came over to help Ronda with her exercises.

"You seem to be healing very well," the therapist said. "I mean it's been a little over a week and already I'm seeing some good range of motion out of the knee. You must be doing your home exercises religiously."

"I am," Ronda said. "The only thing I don't get is why it still hurts like a mother fucker."

"It shouldn't. I mean, there should be some pain, sure. But it shouldn't hurt that bad. Let's do an MRI and see how it looks. I'll set one up for you."

"Thanks. I appreciate it."

❖

Her MRI was scheduled for Wednesday.

"You're so lucky you're a local celebrity," Gayla said as they got ready to go to the appointment. "Do you know how long it takes for normal people to get scheduled for procedures?"

"How long?"

"Longer than two days. That's for sure."

"Well, maybe the demand for MRIs is pretty low right now."

"Maybe, but I doubt it. I think if Ronda Meyers needs something she gets it."

"You don't have to be all pissy about it."

"I'm not. Believe me. I'm just glad I'm on the right side of the toast."

"Smart woman. You're just using me for the perks, huh?"

"Well, that and the sex," Gayla said. "The sex is pretty good."
Ronda laughed.

"That's good to know."

They got Ronda in the car and Gayla drove them to the clinic.

"It seems to be getting better," Gayla commented offhandedly.

"But it's not. It still hurts way more than it should."

"I don't get it. You can use it more, but it hurts still? It doesn't make sense."

They arrived at the clinic and sat in the waiting room waiting to be called in. When they called Ronda's name, Gayla went with her.

"You're not allowed back here, ma'am," the tech said. "We'll take care of her from here."

Ronda looked at Gayla with fear in her eyes, but then got a grip.

"I'll be okay, babe. I'll see you when I'm out of the tube."

The MRI seemed to take forever, and finally the noises stopped and Ronda was moved out from inside the giant tube. The tech helped her off the platform and gave her her crutches.

"You should hear from your doctor within a couple of days," the tech told her.

Ronda and Gayla went out for lunch. After, Ronda took her pain pills.

"You brought them with you?" Gayla said. "It won't be long until we get home."

"I didn't know how bad I'd hurt after the MRI."

"And did you hurt?"

"No more than usual. But it was time so I'm taking them now."

"Okay. It's just that I thought I was in control of your meds and I can't be if you're going to take them whenever."

"I'm not taking them whenever, babe. I just made sure to grab them as we left the house today. It's no biggie."

"Okay. Now, how about you give them to me?"

"I really think I'm okay controlling my meds now, babe. Like I said the other day, it was great for you to do that for me in the beginning, but I can do it now. Really."

Gayla looked unsure for a moment.

"What?" Ronda said.

"Just be careful," Gayla said. "Promise me."

"Be careful, how?"

"Those things are dangerous. I just don't want you getting hooked or anything."

"Oh, please. I'm not going to get hooked."

The nice, easy, peaceful feeling was starting to flow over her. The pills really made her feel good. If only they took away the pain.

"You ready to head home?" Gayla said.

"Sure thing."

Another week passed and Gayla took Ronda in to have her stitches out.

"It's healing very well," the surgeon told them.

"Right on. That's good to hear. But why does it hurt so damned much?" Ronda said.

"It shouldn't. And your MRI results came out wonderfully. You're healing a little ahead of schedule. Your pain should be mostly under control by now."

"Well, it's not. Can I get you to write me another prescription?"

"Sure. If you need it."

Ronda took the slip from him.

"Thank you, sir."

"You're really looking good, Ronda. Keep up the good work."

"When can I use my pool or hot tub?"

"I wouldn't recommend any swimming any time soon. Your therapist will let you know when that's okay to do. You can use your hot tub tomorrow, though."

"Excellent. I've missed soaking in it."

"Just be careful," the doctor said.

"I will."

"If it hurts, get out."

"Yes, sir."

They left and Ronda handed Gayla the prescription.

"Let's go drop this off," she said.

"You still have plenty at home."

"Yeah, but as long as we have the prescription, we should fill it."

"I can put it on the refrigerator door and use it when you get low," Gayla said.

"What's the big deal? Let's just go get it so we'll have it."

"Okay. You win. We'll go get it."

That afternoon, Ronda was tired of the pain. She decided to take three pills instead of just two. She felt good, and the pain was lessened a bit. She thought maybe that's how many she needed to be taking, regardless of doctor's orders.

The next evening, Ronda couldn't wait for dinner to be over.

"What's up with you?" Gayla asked.

"We can go in the hot tub tonight. I'm totally excited."

"God, that'll feel good."

"I know, babe. You do so much around here. I'm sorry I can't do more."

"It's all good. Don't worry about it. It's my pleasure."

"No. You are going to soak in that tub with me tonight and relax for the first time in weeks. I didn't realize how much I was going to need you after that hit."

"Nope. You thought you'd be able to go to the grocery store by yourself and do all normal things around the house. You didn't realize how confining your crutches would be."

"You're right. I didn't. I really appreciate everything you've done. As a matter of fact, I have a question I'd like to ask you."

"What's that?"

"Let's wait until we get in the tub with a couple of drinks."

"You shouldn't drink while you're taking pain pills."

"I'll be fine," Ronda said. "Don't worry. Besides, I'm not due for pills right now."

She didn't tell her she'd just taken some pills about an hour before dinner. She poured them each a scotch then she watched Gayla undress before she helped her get her own clothes off.

"God, you're beautiful," Ronda said.

"I think the pain pills must be messing with your mind." She laughed.

"I've always thought you were beautiful. You know that."

"That's true. And you're drop-dead gorgeous, so we're quite a couple."

"We're one of Houston's power couples to be sure," Ronda said. "Now, let's get in the water."

They went out to the patio and got Ronda in the water. Gayla climbed in after her.

"Oh, yeah. That's what I'm talking about," Gayla said.

"It feels good, doesn't it?"

"Is it too much for your knee?"

"I don't know. It feels good now, but I might have to get out sooner than I'd like. For now, let's just relax and enjoy the evening."

"So what was your question for me?" Gayla said.

"Well, I was thinking…"

"Dangerous."

"Very funny. I'm serious. Gayla, would you move in with me?"

"Wow. This is so not what I expected. But then, I'm practically living with you now."

"You *are* living with me now. So why not make it official? Sell your place and move your stuff over here."

"My stuff wouldn't all fit over here," Gayla said.

"Then we work out a compromise. Some of your stuff goes, some of my stuff goes. It's all good. So what do say?"

"I say that sounds like a lot of work. Why don't we wait until you're off your crutches and then we'll work on it?"

"So that's a yes?"

"It is indeed."

Ronda pulled her to her and kissed her hard on her mouth.

CHAPTER SIXTEEN

Ronda continued to work out with her therapist, eventually moving to the gym to use state-of-the-art equipment.

"You're really doing great," the therapist said.

"It feels like it's doing great, but it still hurts," Ronda said. "Like I almost feel like I could walk on it, but the pain is still out of control."

"That doesn't make any sense. There's no reason for the pain."

"Could you have the doc call me in a prescription for more pills?"

"Sure. I'm sure she won't mind."

"Great. Thanks."

Ronda gave her therapist a different pharmacy to call them in to. One she'd only used a couple of times before. She didn't want anyone denying her the pills since she hurt so badly. They continued working out until the therapist decided Ronda had had enough.

"You keep doing your home exercises. You're definitely getting stronger every time I see you. And I want you to wear this brace now. You shouldn't need your crutches anymore."

"I will. And you'll make sure the doctor calls in a prescription for me?"

"I will."

"Cool. I'll see you in a couple of days."

"Sounds good."

Ronda called Gayla to let her know she was ready to be picked up. She felt that she could drive by then and the therapist thought she could, too, but Gayla was insistent that she drive Ronda everywhere.

While she waited for Gayla, she wandered out to the practice field. She watched the team scrimmage and felt a loneliness in the pit of her stomach. Would she ever be able to play again? Everyone seemed so hopeful. Everyone seemed to think she'd be on the field next season. But did they really believe that? Or was it all just lip service meant to make her feel better?

Either way, she was determined to work as hard as she could, as hard as her knee would let her. It really didn't make sense. She could see her range of motion improving, but still she hurt. She shouldn't be hurting if she was improving. It was a contradiction. But she couldn't change how she felt.

Gayla came onto the field to join her.

"How do they look?" Gayla said.

"Weak in the cornerback position."

"Of course they do. Nobody can replace you, Ronda. You were league MVP last year. No one can step in and fill those shoes. They just have to do the best they do. And Lagerman is no slacker out there. She looks good."

"I don't know about that. But I guess it doesn't really matter anyway. I'm not out there to help the team so she's all they've got."

"You keep doing all you're doing and you'll be out there next year, better than ever."

"That's the goal."

"Keep your eye on it."

"Oh, that reminds me. I want to stop by CVS on the way home."

"What's there?" Gayla asked.

"Doc called in a prescription for me."

"What kind of prescription?"

"Pain pills. I'm almost out and I didn't know if the surgeon would refill me again. And my knee's still killing me."

"That's some dangerous business you're getting into. Having two doctors calling in pain pills to two pharmacies just sounds like trouble. Are you sure you know what you're doing?"

"It's all good, babe. It's just a precaution in case the surgeon won't refill them again."

"Maybe he thinks you should be off them by now," Gayla said.

"Well, that's not going to happen. Not until the pain goes away."

"And when is that going to happen? Everyone says you're getting better. Why are you still hurting?"

"No one seems to know. They all think the pain should be gone by now. But it's not."

"Okay. We'll pick up your pain pills. But I still don't feel good about this."

They got home and Ronda took some pills.

"Don't you need food with those?" Gayla said.

"I've found that they don't bother me. And I'm really sore after my therapy. Hey, you want to hit the hot tub?"

"Sure. Let's go."

They soaked in the tub for a while until Ronda couldn't stand it any longer.

"I love being out here with you," she said.

"Thanks, baby. I enjoy it, too."

"But it always makes me want to get you out of the tub and into my bed."

"We'll get there, baby. For now, let's just relax."

Ronda was relaxed. If there was one thing those pain pills did for her, they made her relaxed and at ease. She didn't stress as much about things right after she'd taken them. She was with Gayla and life was good.

She slipped her arm around Gayla and just soaked in the tub. The streams of jets felt so good against her muscles. Before she knew it, she was drifting off. She awoke to Gayla shaking her.

"Ronda! Ronda! Wake up!"

"What? Huh? I'm awake."

"You fell asleep in the hot tub. Not a good idea. You were sinking. I don't know that I could have pulled you out. You need to be more careful."

"Sorry. I guess I relaxed too much."

"I guess. Maybe we shouldn't mix your pain pills with the hot tub."

"I don't know about that. Maybe. We'll see."

"No. I don't think 'we'll see' is an answer. I'm not willing to risk you drowning, Ronda."

"It's probably a combination of things. Not necessarily the pain pills's fault."

"Still. I'd rather you not take them before we use the hot tub," Gayla said. "Now, let's get out of here."

Ronda was unsteady as Gayla helped her out of the tub. They got her out and, still light-headed, she sat on one of the lounge chairs.

"I'm sorry," she said.

"Huh?"

"For scaring you. I'm sorry."

"It's okay. My heart's starting to beat normally again."

Ronda had to admit she was not feeling the usual euphoria the pills gave her. She told herself it was just because of the scare. She would feel fine soon enough.

"So, I'm guessing sex is out?"

"I'm thinking I need to make you some dinner. I told you not to take those pills on an empty stomach."

"You really need to lighten up on the pills. They're not the devil's making. They help me. I can't imagine not having them."

"And I don't want you to go without. I just want you to take them as directed," Gayla said.

Ronda said nothing in her defense. She knew if Gayla knew she was taking three at a time instead of two, there'd be hell to pay.

"Okay. I'll work on that. In the meantime, I'll hang out here while you fix dinner, okay?"

Ronda lay back on the lounge and closed her eyes. She was tired. Apparently, physical therapy was too much for her. It must have pushed her too hard. Not that she couldn't take it. She could. It just wiped her out. She relaxed into the lounge and fell asleep. She awoke once again to Gayla lightly shaking her.

"Ronda? Dinner's ready. Wake up."

Ronda was awake but felt a little cloudy in her head.

"I'm awake," she said.

"You sure? You gonna stay awake?"

"Yeah. I'm up." She started to feel more clearheaded. "I'm awake. Can you help me off this lounge chair? Dinner smells great and I'm so ready to taste it."

They got Ronda to a standing position. They got her knee brace on and Gayla handed her her crutches.

"You feeling okay?" Gayla said.

"Sure. Why?"

"Your color is a little off."

"My color doesn't go off. I'm always the same color. I can't be pale. Or gray. Or whatever. It's just your imagination."

"I suppose you may be right. Okay. Well, if you're all right, then let's go eat."

She led the way into the house and served dinner while Ronda got situated in her chair. As they ate, Ronda again brought up the subject of them living together.

"I can't wait until I'm off these crutches," she said.

"I'm sure they're a hassle. But they seem necessary. When should you get off them?"

"I don't know," Ronda lied. The thought of no crutches scared her. She still felt she needed them. "Still. I want to be able to move independently so we can get your stuff moved in here. I can't wait to have us living together."

"You're so sweet," Gayla said. "I'm glad you still want to."

"Of course. Why wouldn't I?"

"I don't know. I wondered if it was in the heat of passion that you originally suggested it."

"Nope. It was a carefully thought out question. I really want you living with me. It only makes sense. We're always together anyway. And I love having you with me all the time."

"You don't have to sell it to me again. I already said yes."

"I know. I just feel like I may need to remind you of what a great thing it will be once in a while."

"Well, you don't. I'm on board with this idea one hundred percent."

"Right on."

"Now, you sit tight while I do the dishes."

"Sounds good."

Ronda shifted in her seat so she could watch Gayla move about the kitchen. She was so gorgeous with such a kickass figure that Ronda couldn't keep her eyes off her. She felt bad that she couldn't help, but she was pretty useless on her crutches. She felt uncoordinated on them. But she was hoping to be off them soon. She was working hard toward that goal.

Gayla finished the dishes and came back to the table to join Ronda.

"So, what now, baby? You want to watch some television or something?"

"No. I want you. I've been asking for you for hours. Let me have you now?"

"How can a girl possibly say no to you?"

"That's what I was hoping you would say."

As was now customary those days, their dance toward the bed was anything but romantic. But Ronda had gotten more self-sufficient at taking her brace off and maneuvering herself on the bed. Still, it didn't flow smoothly. Rather than a fine-tuned ballet, it was more like a rusty robot. But they got there and when flesh met flesh, nothing else mattered.

They lay facing each other and Ronda ran her hand over Gayla's skin.

"I love your skin. It's like porcelain against mine," Ronda said. "And it's so soft and smooth."

"You're skin's pretty soft too for such a tough gal."

Ronda laughed.

"I'm not tough."

"Tell that to your opponents."

"Well, maybe on the football field," Ronda said.

"Definitely on the football field."

"But not in bed."

"No. In bed you're not rough or tough. You're smooth as silk."

"Mm. Come here. Let me kiss you," Ronda said.

Gayla lifted her mouth and Ronda traced it with her thumb. Then she lowered her lips and brushed against her.

"You're making me crazy," Gayla said.

"Patience, my dear."

"I don't have any."

She pulled Ronda to her and kissed her hard on the mouth. She ran her tongue over Ronda's lips until Ronda had no choice but to open them and allow Gayla's tongue inside. Her clit swelled at the feel of their tongues meeting. She rolled over on top of Gayla and did her best to grind into her.

"Careful," Gayla said. "I don't want you to hurt yourself."

"But I need to be with you, against you, in you."

"I want all those things, too. Just do them carefully, please."

Ronda slid off Gayla and used her hand rather than her body to convey everything she was feeling. She moved her hand all over her body, softly, slowly. She was crazy about Gayla and she wanted to leave no doubt in her mind about that.

"Do you know how I feel about you?" she whispered in her ear.

"Tell me."

"I'm crazy about you. I can't wait until we can live together, show the world we're a couple."

"Oh, baby. I know what you mean. I can't wait either."

"I want to live with you forever, babe."

"I want that, too."

"Good. Thank God."

She kissed Gayla again, ferociously. She needed Gayla to know how crazy she was about her. Words weren't enough. She placed her hand on Gayla's breast as they kissed and she kneaded it. It was full and firm and felt so wonderful in her hand. She took the nipple and pinched it softly at first, then a little harder until Gayla cried out as she came.

"I love that you come to breast play."

"Baby, just being with you gets me so excited. You tweak my nipples and kiss me, and I'm over the moon."

"Mm. I'm glad." She lowered her head and licked Gayla's other nipple. She sucked as much of her breast in her mouth as she could and continued to flick her tongue over her nipple.

Gayla placed her hands on Ronda's head and held it in place. Her breathing became labored and Ronda knew she was close. She sucked harder and licked faster, and finally, Gayla screamed as her orgasm cascaded over her.

"Baby, you sure know how to love me."

"I love doing it. You're so easy to please."

Ronda placed her hand between Gayla's legs.

"Oh, yeah. You're so nice and wet for me."

"How could I not be? I've already had two orgasms."

"Very true," Ronda said.

She slipped her fingers inside Gayla.

"Oh, babe. You're so smooth and soft. You feel so good. You like that?"

Gayla could only moan. Ronda took that as a yes.

"Oh, yeah. I'm gonna make you feel so good," Ronda said.

She moved her fingers in and out, over and over until Gayla was grinding her hips into her. Ronda knew she wanted release. She found that special spot she knew always worked for her and barely stroked it, but that was all it took. Gayla cried out her name and held her close as she rode wave after wave of orgasm.

When she had quit spasming on Ronda, Ronda slowly slid her hand out. She rested her head on the pillow with Gayla's.

"You're so much fun," she said.

"So are you. I love the way you make love to me." She propped herself up on an elbow. "But now it's time for me to make love to you."

"Be careful of my knee."

"Don't worry, I will. This is about pleasure, not pain."

She kissed Ronda, a soft, gentle kiss. The tenderness of it sent shockwaves throughout Ronda's body. Gayla kissed down her chest to her breast. She sucked and licked Ronda's nipple and breast, much as Ronda had done hers. She continued to suck and flick, but Ronda didn't climax. Ronda didn't come from nipple play. She was waiting for the main attraction.

Gayla kissed lower, down Ronda's tight stomach until she could climb between her legs. Ronda tensed briefly.

"Watch my knee," she said.

"I told you. I'll be careful."

Gayla spread Ronda's right leg out, but left her left leg there. Ronda moved it as far as she could comfortably. Then Gayla lowered her mouth to Ronda. She licked all over her, from her center to her clit and back again. She plunged her tongue as deep as it would go and moved it around inside her. Then she licked back to her clit, which she circled several times before placing her tongue directly on it. While she worked it with her tongue, she slipped her fingers inside.

Ronda's head was spinning from all the sensations. She thought she would explode. She needed to explode. She closed her eyes and focused on nothing but Gayla. She saw colors on her eyelids. The colors got more intense until they exploded like fireworks as she felt her body release into climax after climax. It took her a moment before she was able to speak.

"Holy shit, babe. That was amazing," Ronda said.

"Mm. I enjoyed it."

"Get up here and let me kiss you."

Gayla climbed up next to Ronda, who kissed her lightly.

"Can you imagine? We get to do this every day of our lives?" Ronda said.

"I know. It's going to be fantastic. Heck, it already is."

"Yeah, it is. You know, I was thinking. We could have some of the women from the team move your stuff since I still can't."

"Maybe. It just seems like such a personal thing, you know? To move in with someone else? I just feel like I'd rather we do it together when you can. I'm not going anywhere until then, baby."

"I suppose that's true."

"It is." She kissed Ronda again. "It most definitely is."

CHAPTER SEVENTEEN

Ronda continued to improve with each therapy appointment. Her therapist told her she was way ahead of the curve. But the fact that she complained of pain still had them concerned. She was starting to feel better, but still had some sharp pains. All her tests showed she was fine and should be pain free at that point. The team doctor continued to prescribe her Vicodin for her pain, but warned her he would soon have to stop.

Ronda didn't want him to stop. She was glad she was healing, but the pills made her feel so good. She didn't want to quit taking them. She was up to four at a time, so they went faster than they should. She worried someone would notice. She had started having follow up appointments with her regular doctor as well. She also prescribed the pills for Ronda, but also said she would have to quit doing it soon.

The thought of no more pills made Ronda uptight. She couldn't stand the thought of not having them. She needed them. Whether she had pain or not, she needed the pills. She knew it and knew no one else could possibly understand.

Sure, the pills made her a little groggy sometimes. That was half the fun of them, losing herself in them. She was careful not to take them right before the hot tub again. But she found that two pills and a couple of glasses of scotch could mellow her right out. And she liked being mellow. It was a nice feeling, being relieved of all her stress and worries about whether she'd ever play again. She didn't want to give that up.

It had been eight weeks since she tore her ACL. The season was over. She should be out selling houses. She and Gayla talked to her doctor about that.

"Is there any reason I can't show houses?" she asked.

"None that I can think of," Dr. Martin said. "Just make sure Gayla is with you. You're still taking Vicodin and I don't want you driving on it."

"No worries. She's my chauffeur."

"I just think it would do wonders for her mental health," Gayla said.

"I'm sure it would," Dr. Martin said. "And you're doing great work, so don't overdo it. I wouldn't show houses the same days as physical therapy. That kind of thing."

"No. I won't. I'll take it easy on PT days. They hurt and wear me out, anyway."

"I think we need to talk about your Vicodin," Dr. Martin said.

"I agree," Gayla said.

"Whoa. What is this? A double-team?"

"I'm just concerned. You shouldn't still need them at this stage in your recovery."

"But I do. I hurt and they help."

"But do they?" Gayla said. "Or is it all in your head?"

"No. I assure you. It's all in my knee."

"Okay. I'll write you another script. I want you to come back in a month so we can reevaluate you, okay?"

"Thanks, Doc."

They got out to the car. Ronda was fuming.

"What the fuck was that in there?" she said.

"What? I had a concern, so I voiced it."

"You blindsided me and made me look like a chump. You couldn't have discussed this with me before today if you had issues with it?"

"I meant to, but the opportunity never came up. As soon as she brought it up, I thought I should mention my concerns as well."

"Well, I appreciate that you feel it necessary to monitor my med use, but as I've told you time and time again, I've got it under control. I'll worry about how many pills I take and when. It's of no concern to you."

"I disagree. I think it is of concern to me. You're my girlfriend, so I'm allowed to worry about you."

"You should be worried that I'm in pain. Which the pills help with. You shouldn't worry about the pills."

"Okay. I'm sorry. I'll try not to be concerned with your pills."

"Thank you. Now let's stop and get some dinner."

They ate dinner and discussed the business of showing houses.

"I'm going to need you to get my name back out there," Ronda said. "You need to let people know the season is over and I'm back."

"I think they'll probably know that. But I'll get us some houses. Don't you worry. I suppose I'll have to get all single-story homes to begin with, huh?"

"No. There's no money in them. I want to stick with Upper Kirby and River Oaks. I can have you accompany the people upstairs."

"But I'm not an agent."

"You're my assistant. Therefore, you can help me by walking people upstairs."

"But I usually move on to the next house as soon as you get there."

"That just won't work. Besides, I'll be riding with you, remember?"

"Oh, yes," Gayla said. "That's right."

"So, we'll have to change our way of doing things anyway. We'll get a system worked out."

After dinner, Gayla drove them home and they climbed in the hot tub. Gayla sidled up to Ronda.

"So, are you still mad at me?"

"A little."

"Aw, come on, baby." She dragged her hand across Ronda's shoulders and down her arm. "I didn't mean any harm by it. I swear."

"Oh, shit. Now you got my body all on alert when my mind is still not amused."

"Let it go, baby. Don't stay mad." She brushed her breasts against Ronda's arm.

Ronda shifted slightly to face Gayla.

"Just stay out of my pill business, okay?"

"Okay. Now, kiss me?"

Ronda cupped Gayla's jaw in her hand. She lowered her mouth to take Gayla's lips in hers.

"How was that?" she said.

"Nice. But you can do better."

Ronda kissed her hard and pried her lips open with her tongue. She allowed her tongue to languidly enter and dance slowly with Gayla's. She broke the kiss.

"You're driving me crazy," Gayla said.

"Good. You deserve it."

"I'm sorry. I said I was sorry. I promised not to meddle anymore. Now please."

Ronda pulled her close and kissed her hard. This time she guided her tongue all over the inside of Gayla's mouth. Gayla's tongue followed hers and they danced a dance of lust.

"Oh, Jesus, what you do to me," Ronda said. "I can't get enough of you."

Gayla took Ronda's hand and placed it between her legs.

"Please," she said. "I need you."

Ronda caressed Gayla's silky softness. She teased her as she dragged her hand from one end to the other. She slipped her fingers inside and ran them along her satin walls. She plunged them as deep as they could go. Gayla moved on her fingers. Ronda knew she was close. She took her fingers out and rubbed her clit until Gayla buried her face in Ronda's shoulder to keep from crying out too loudly.

"You are such a good lover," Gayla said. "I suppose I shouldn't think of all those poor, heartbroken girls you practiced on to get such a perfect technique."

Ronda laughed.

"Who says they were heartbroken? Did it ever occur to you that I might have been the heartbroken one?"

"I thought you kept your heart protected."

"I did. But only after Serena."

"But you were in high school."

"Still, she taught me everything I know."

"I just find that odd," Gayla said. "You were so young."

"I was. She wasn't."

"What? I thought she was like your best friend or something."

"She was. Just older than I was. She was the neighbor's daughter. She'd just separated from her partner and moved back home."

"How old was she? Because I'm thinking I'm going to be extremely pissed off at her."

"She was thirty-one."

"That's too old to be messing around with a seventeen-year-old."

"So I learned. But at the time, it was fun and she taught me everything I know," Ronda said.

"Well, I'm grateful to her for that." Gayla moved close to Ronda. "But I think it was wrong that she was toying with your affection."

"Look at it this way. If she hadn't, I wouldn't have been so guarded and might not have been available when it was time for you and me to get together."

"Don't you dare defend her or what she did to you. She hurt you. Don't you forget that."

"I don't forget that, babe. Don't worry. But she taught me how to please a woman. So, when I'm making love to you, I do it with skills I learned from her."

"Suddenly, the mood is gone. Let's get out of the tub. Maybe watch a movie or something."

"Hey, babe. What's up? Please don't be that way."

"No, seriously. The mood is definitely gone. I'm sorry, Ronda. I just can't imagine a thirty-one-year-old messing around with a seventeen-year-old kid. And no one knew? No one did a damned thing about it?"

"We kept it a secret. And as for me being seventeen, did it ever occur to you I might have been hot?"

"I've no doubt you were hot," Gayla said. "But still…she should have kept her hands to herself. When was the last time you heard from her?"

"When she got a job and moved away. I begged her to take me with her, but she wouldn't."

"Of course not. You needed to finish high school and go on to college."

"I know this now. But at the time, all I wanted was to be with her."

"So she broke your heart, but it was in your best interest."

"Yeah."

"I'm sorry she hurt you, baby," Gayla said.

"Thanks. So am I."

"Do you ever try to find her?"

"Every once in a while I'll get a wild hair and search for her online or on social network sites, but I've yet to find her."

"It's probably for the best. She's probably all old and gray now."

Ronda laughed.

"You are so funny. I bet she's a fine specimen of a middle-aged woman."

"So if you found her, should I be nervous?" Gayla said.

"Hell no. You're mine now. I'm yours. That's all that matters."

"Good answer."

"Thanks. Now are you sure we need to get out of the hot tub?" Ronda moved in and kissed Gayla again.

"I really think we should get out of the water."

"But why? I'm thinking it's time for round two."

"I'd love that. But out of the hot tub. We've been in here long enough."

Gayla stood by as Ronda climbed out, then she climbed out.

"You've gotten so much better at your mobility," Gayla said.

"I should hope so. I'm worried with therapy dropping to twice a week that I won't continue to improve, though."

"I'm sure you will. And if your improvement slows down, I'm sure they'll up you back to three times."

"I suppose that's true."

"I'm also impressed at how much your balance has improved."

"It's all in the work we're doing, babe. It might be hard work, but it's worth it."

"Good." Gayla gingerly leaned into Ronda and kissed her. "I can't wait until there's no more restrictions on you."

"Neither can I, babe."

They walked to the bedroom where Ronda lay back on the bed.

"Come here, lover."

"Lover? I like the sound of that."

"That reminds me," Ronda said. "How should I introduce you? Lover? Girlfriend?"

"How about partner?"

"Whoa that just gave me the heebie-jeebies."

"Are you serious? Because if you're not serious about us, then I can definitely scale back the services I perform for you."

"No...no, no. I'm serious about you. About us. It's just that partner is such a strong word."

"Baby, I'm going to be *living* with you."

"I know."

"So, don't you think partner is appropriate?" Gayla said.

"Yeah. I suppose it is. So, you're my partner. Wow. I have a partner."

"Yes, you do," Gayla said. "Indeed you do."

Gayla climbed up and straddled Ronda.

"And your partner wants to make love to you," she said. She bent over and kissed her as she rubbed her clit against Ronda's belly.

"Well, I'd say that's one of the perks of having a partner," Ronda said when the kiss ended.

"Indeed it is."

Gayla kissed Ronda's cheek and neck. She sucked her earlobe, all the while rubbing herself all over her.

"Oh, shit," Ronda said. "You're getting me all wet."

Gayla reached behind her and felt between Ronda's legs.

"So I am."

"That's not what I meant."

"Oh, you mean the wet from me?" Gayla said.

"Yeah. It's sexy as fuck."

Gayla reached between her legs and got her fingers wet. She wiped them on Ronda's lips, then slipped them in her mouth. Ronda licked them clean.

"Oh, dear God. You're trying to kill me, aren't you?" she said.

"Just trying to get you in the mood.

"I'm in the mood. Trust me on that."

"Good." She moved down Ronda's body until she could take a nipple in her mouth.

"Mm," Ronda said. "That feels so good."

Gayla switched to Ronda's other nipple, all the while grinding herself into her.

"You've got to be getting as worked up as I am," Ronda said.

"I am. Don't worry about that."

"Well, how can you concentrate on me? Maybe you should let me have my way with you."

"And interrupt what I'm doing? No way."

Gayla moved farther down until she was straddling Ronda's hips. She rubbed her own clit. As she did so, she dipped her hand down and rubbed Ronda's. Ronda propped herself up on her elbows to watch Gayla touch herself, but soon was overwhelmed with feelings as Gayla rubbed her clit, too. She was getting close, but wanted to hold off and make Gayla come first.

"Are you close?" Ronda said.

"Oh, yeah. You?"

"Fuck yeah. Come, babe, so I can come."

"You go first."

"Never."

Ronda held on. It wasn't easy. Each stroke made her teeter on the edge, but she was determined to make Gayla climax first.

"Please," Ronda said. "Please come for me. I want to come seeing your face lost in the pleasure. Come on, babe."

Gayla stroked them both harder and faster. She leaned back and Ronda could see everything about her that made her a woman. She closed her eyes and grabbed Ronda's upper thigh.

"Oh, God," she said. "Oh, my God, Ronda."

That was all Ronda needed. Her climax was hard and deep. She felt it down to her toes.

"Damn, babe. I mean, holy shit. That was awesome."

"Yes, it was." Gayla rolled off of Ronda and settled against her. Ronda was exhausted. She fell fast asleep. She awoke the next morning to the smell of coffee brewing. She was usually awake before Gayla. She wondered what was up. She went into the bathroom and took a few pain pills to start the day. Then went out to see what Gayla was doing.

"What are you doing up so early?" she said.

"I figured vacation is over."

"Vacation? Is that what this pain filled hell has been?"

"You know what I mean. We got you cleared to start showing houses again, so let's get to it. I've been looking at properties. There are quite a few out there. We just need to build our clientele. So I'll spend this morning calling former clients to see if they know anyone who needs a house. Meanwhile, you can update your website. Let them know you're back at it after a slight hiatus. We're going to be busy today."

"Wow. I'm going to need some coffee." Her head felt a little light from the pills, which was good. It was the feeling she enjoyed. Working on her website would be easy. And fun. And hopefully, profitable.

She poured them each a cup of coffee and they set about their business. A few hours later, Ronda took some more pain pills. They had lunch and got back to work. Ronda was feeling no pain and sat staring at her screen.

"How's that website going?" Gayla asked.

"Huh? Oh, it's going great, why?"

"Because you've been spacing out for fifteen minutes now."

"I have? Sorry. I'm working on it, though."

"Okay."

"How are the phone calls going?" Ronda asked.

"I've gotten five referrals so far. I've called and have them scheduled for later this week and next."

"Most excellent. It'll feel good to be busy again."

"Yes, it will. I've got the rundowns on the prospects. I'll give them to you before we meet with them, just like before. And I'll be there to help if you need anything at all. Don't try to be a tough guy, okay? If you need help, ask for it. I've already explained to them that you're recovering from an injury, though most of them had already heard that, it being the biggest news of the season."

"Yeah, I'd imagine it was. I can't wait until I heal and can move around more and be more independent. You've got to be getting tired of taking care of me all the time."

"I like to think I'll still be taking care of you even after you've healed," Gayla said.

"To a degree. But not like you have to now."

"We'll just see about that. Who do you think has taken care of you all these years before your injury, Miss Thing?"

"I suppose that is the truth. You do a hell of a lot for me. And I appreciate it."

"And when I'm living here, I'll still be cooking and cleaning, though I will expect some help."

"Yeah," Ronda said. "I'll be happy to help once I'm off these crutches."

"I know you will. And that day will come."

Chapter Eighteen

It was time to show the first house. Ronda took some pills just to take the edge off. She was actually a little nervous. The pills helped with that. Now she was unstoppable. She would sell this house, no problem.

Gayla ran down the high points to push to the couple. Ronda did her best to commit them to her memory. She felt a little foggy. She had a soda. That should help clear her mind.

"Are you okay?" Gayla asked.

"Yeah. I'm fine, why?"

"You don't look good. Your eyes look spacey."

"My eyes look what? You're paranoid. I'm good. We're good. Let's rock this sale."

The young couple arrived and Ronda went off-script. She worked the couple like she thought she should, but in the end, the couple said they weren't interested. Maybe if Ronda had another house to show them sometime, she should let them know.

Once they were gone, Gayla was in her face.

"What the hell was that?"

"Was what? So they weren't interested. So, what?"

"You didn't bring up a single point I told you to make. If you had, we might have had a sale."

"You think it's so easy, get your license and do it yourself."

"We've been through this. Our teamwork is so great. I don't need a license. But you need to listen to me. What the hell is wrong with you? You acted like you'd never shown a house before."

"Jeez, woman. Back off. So I missed a sale. It's bound to happen. Nobody is a hundred percent. So I'm a little rusty. It'll all come back to me."

"When was the last time you took a pain pill?"

"My knee doesn't hurt."

"That's not what I asked. When did you take your pills?"

"What's it matter to you? I'm in charge of my pills."

"I'm willing to bet you just took them before you showed this house," Gayla said. "I think they confuse you and make it hard for you to think straight. Maybe we should postpone selling houses until you're off them."

Getting off the pills was the last thing Ronda wanted to think about. Okay, so maybe she was a little too foggy when she showed the house. Maybe she should have waited until the initial buzz wore off. But she hadn't. She knew better now and would make sure to time it better in the future.

"I'm fine. Now, let's go to the second house."

This time, she focused hard on everything Gayla told her to use as selling points. She committed everything to memory and when the buyers got there, she was on her game. They sold the house and were both in an excellent mood as the buyers left.

"See? I told you I'd get my groove back," Ronda said.

"Still, it was sad to see you at that first house. It was like watching a rookie. Not what I like to see from you."

"So now I'm fifty percent. Batting five hundred. It's not a horrible way to start back in the business. Let's go to The V to have a drink to celebrate."

"When did you last take your pills?" Gayla asked.

"Who cares? I nailed it. See? You need to not worry about my medications."

"I do worry about them if we're going to go out for a drink."

"They don't interfere with my drinking. Besides, I'm not driving."

"I'm not worried about you driving. It's more you passing out and me having to keep you from falling to the floor that I worry about."

"Don't. I'm fine."

"You took pills before you showed that first house, didn't you?"

"Let's not start that again. The point is, it's been long enough since I've taken them that I can easily have a celebratory drink. Now, come on."

They got in the car and drove in silence to The V. By the time they got out of the car, Ronda's celebratory mood was fading fast.

"Look, Gayla, we just made a nice sale today. It'll bring us big bank. So, relax and enjoy it. Don't be so uptight. Please. This should be a time of celebrating, not complaining."

"I'm sorry. It's just that I worry about you. And as your partner, I'm allowed to do that."

"Fair enough, babe. Fair enough." She kissed her lightly and they went inside. The place was busier than it had been on previous visits, but it still wasn't packed.

"So, Thursday night is when things start hoppin' here, huh?" Ronda asked the bartender.

"Yeah. Give us a few hours and it'll be wall-to-wall in here."

"Well, we won't be staying that long. How about a couple of scotches?"

"Coming right up."

"God, it feels good to be back in the game," Ronda said to Gayla.

"Yes, it does. That second couple was a slam dunk."

"Yeah, they were. You do such a good job letting me know exactly what they want to hear, babe. I'll never go off script again like I did in the first house today."

"I hope not."

"I won't. I don't know what came over me."

Gayla gave her a questioning look.

"I swear," Ronda said. "I don't."

But Ronda did know. And she knew Gayla was right. She couldn't take her pills right before she showed a house. That had cost her the sale. She believed that. But she would never admit that to Gayla. She didn't need to know. To suspect was bad enough. And Ronda knew she didn't have a problem with her medications, regardless of what Gayla kept hinting at. She took them to ease the pain, to make things better. There was nothing wrong with that.

They had a second drink and chatted about the houses they would show the following week. Ronda had physical therapy the next day, so house showing was out. And then it was the weekend.

"We should do something this weekend. Maybe get away to the beach or something," Ronda said.

"Is salt water okay for your knee?"

"I can ask. I don't need to go in the water anyway. I can kick back with a six-pack and watch you frolic."

"That does sound nice. It's a quick getaway, but I think we've earned it. You talk to your therapist tomorrow and find out what she says."

Ronda talked to her therapist who told her she needed to be careful in the waves. Her knee wasn't strong enough to withstand the pounding of them against it. She could wade out into the shallow water, though.

"Right on. That's great news," Ronda said. "I think we'll head down tonight, right, Gayla?"

"I'll step outside right now to see if we can get a room," Gayla said.

When Gayla was out of earshot, Ronda asked about more pills.

"Hey, is there any way the doctor can call in another prescription?" she asked. "I'm running out again."

"Has it already been a month?" her therapist said.

"If not, pretty close."

"I'll ask her to call something in for you. How bad is the pain?"

"It's not like it's constant anymore, but when it flares up, it really rears its ugly head."

"Okay. I'll let her know. Hopefully, she'll call in some more Vicodin. Although, I think you need to talk to her about maybe getting off of them."

"Yeah. I'm sure soon I'll be able to."

"Okay."

They finished their appointment and Ronda walked outside to find Gayla grinning ear to ear.

"What?"

"I got us a condo for the weekend. We have it until Monday morning."

"And when do we check in?"

"This afternoon. Let's go pack."

They went home and got ready for the weekend. Ronda even made sure to pack their new toys. They were on the road by two thirty and checked into their condo by four and unpacked by four thirty.

"Let's go to the water," Ronda said.

"Remember what she said," Gayla said. "Don't get out in the waves."

"I won't."

They went down to the water and Ronda made herself comfortable in a beach chair while Gayla immediately got wet. Ronda watched happily as Gayla played in the waves. She wanted to get in there and play with her, but wasn't about to risk her knee. Then she got an idea. She could say she hurt her knee in the waves. That way no one would question continuing to give her Vicodin. She thought it was a brilliant, failsafe idea.

Gayla came out of the water and placed her hands on Ronda's armrests and dripped water all over her. She leaned in and kissed her.

"Mm. Salt," Ronda said.

"Is that a bad thing?"

"Not at all. Kiss me again. This time like you mean it."

Gayla did kiss her, a passionate kiss that rained salt water all over Ronda.

"Like that?" she said.

"Yeah, like that."

Ronda looked up at Gayla and enjoyed the view of her cleavage in her swimsuit. She had a knockout figure and seeing her in her suit got Ronda's juices flowing.

"You're so fucking hot," Ronda said.

"I'm glad you think so."

"I really do. You ready to go back to the room?"

"No. I'm going back in the water."

"You're killing me."

"Relax and enjoy it."

Ronda did enjoy watching Gayla's ass as she walked back to the water. She was a fine specimen of a woman, and Ronda was ready to take her to bed. She didn't know how long Gayla would make her wait, but she hoped it wouldn't be too long. She opened another beer and watched Gayla play.

This time when Gayla came out of the water, she grabbed a towel and towel dried her hair before drying off the rest of her.

"Do you do that on purpose? Just to make me crazy?" Ronda said.

"Do what?"

"You know. Bend over and dry off like that."

"I'm just drying off. Not in any particular way."

"I don't know," Ronda said. "You look hella sexy with your leg on the chair and your cleavage on display."

"I need to get dry. Turbo down a little." She laughed.

"I'm trying, but you're driving me mad."

"Well, let's get back to the room then. I need a shower before we go get dinner."

"Yeah. A shower sounds wonderful."

"You didn't even get in the water," Gayla said.

"No, but I got sand on me. And I'd hate to have to have you shower alone."

"Yes, that would be a travesty, wouldn't it?"

"Indeed it would."

They went back up to their room and stripped out of their sun wear. Gayla stepped into the shower and Ronda followed close behind.

"You really are covered in sand," Ronda said. "Here. Let me help you get some of that off you."

She rubbed soap into the washcloth and gently dragged it over the skin on Gayla's back.

"Tell me if I'm hurting you. I don't want to grate your skin off with the sand."

"No. It feels wonderful." She leaned back into Ronda.

Ronda moved the washcloth to Gayla's shoulders and then down her front to caress her breasts. She kissed her neck.

"I want to make sure I'm getting you nice and clean," she said.

"You're doing a wonderful job."

"Mm. And what's this?" Ronda spun Gayla around and slid the washcloth between her legs.

Gayla placed her hands on Ronda's shoulders to brace herself.

"That area needs special attention," she said.

Ronda hung up the washcloth and returned her hand to Gayla's wet center. She slipped her fingers inside while she kissed where her neck met her shoulder.

"Oh, God, Ronda. The things you make me feel."

"Yeah? You like that?"

"God yes. You feel amazing."

"Good. So do you."

She took her fingers out and rubbed them on Gayla's swollen clit.

"Oh, God, Ronda. Oh, God, yes!"

Ronda held tightly to her so she wouldn't fall.

"Oh, my God. That was awesome," Gayla said.

"I'm glad you enjoyed it."

"Dear God, yes. Now let's get out of this shower."

"What about me?" Ronda said.

"It's not safe in here for you. But don't worry. You're about to get yours."

"Most excellent. I like the way that sounds."

They climbed out and dried off and Ronda grabbed her crutches and walked to the bedroom. Gayla was right behind her.

"You're so hot," Gayla said. "Have I mentioned that lately?"

"I'm losing some of my form. I need to work out harder and more often."

"You need to do what you need to do to keep that knee safe."

"Yeah, but why can't I work out the rest of my body? I don't want to get all flabby."

"You don't need to worry about that. But why not ask your therapist?"

"I think I will," Ronda said.

She was lying on the bed then, waiting for Gayla to join her.

"You're just so luscious. I never know where to start," Gayla said.

"I've got a few ideas."

"Really? Where?"

"Right here." Ronda spread her lower lips.

"Right here?" Gayla dragged her hand over her.

"Yep."

"Mm. Okay."

Gayla knelt on the end of the bed and buried her face between Ronda's legs. She licked and sucked and lapped at all she found there. Ronda placed her hand on the back of Gayla's head and moved against her until she lost all thoughts save the feelings Gayla was eliciting. She closed her eyes and rode out the waves that rushed over her.

"I should take another shower," Ronda said.

"Nah. You'll be fine. Let's go. I'm starving."

They went out to dinner at a small tavern. The dinner was great and the service was pleasant.

"She is totally flirting with you," Gayla said about their waitress.

"She's not."

"She is."

"Even if she was, who cares? I'm with you."

"Prove it."

"What do you mean?" Ronda asked.

"Hold my hand."

"Here in Galveston? That could get us shot."

"Just the next time she comes by."

"Fine. I didn't realize you were the jealous kind."

"I don't like to see someone flirting with my woman," Gayla said. "That's a normal reaction."

"I don't blame you, but she wasn't flirting with me."

"Here she comes," Gayla said. "Hold my hand."

Ronda reached across the table and took Gayla's hand. She smiled as the waitress set down their two drinks.

"Can I get you anything else?" the waitress said.

"Nope. I think we're good. Thanks, though," Ronda said.

The waitress walked away.

"See? No flirting," Ronda said.

"I'm still not convinced."

"Babe, it's only you for me. I don't notice other women. I swear."

"Well, thank you for holding my hand."

"You need to know," Ronda said. "Any time I don't isn't because I don't want to, it's because I don't think it's safe."

"I suppose that makes sense. I'm sorry I was jealous. But she was flirting."

"Let her. Let 'em all. You're the only one for me."

"You're so sweet. And smooth."

Ronda laughed.

"I mean it, babe."

"Okay. I concede. So what's on the agenda for after dinner?"

"I thought we'd go for a walk on the beach."

"Is that safe? I mean, can you maneuver your knee?"

"I did just fine earlier today didn't I?" Ronda said.

"Yes, but you didn't have to go far."

"You might be right. So, skip the walk on the beach. We'll go back to our place, climb into the Jacuzzi tub and just relax the night away."

Chapter Nineteen

The rest of the weekend passed wonderfully. They spent their time making love and playing in the water. Ronda was very careful not to get in the waves, and Gayla got out in them and dove in and out of them like a fish. Ronda spent a lot of time in her beach chair on the sand watching Gayla.

They spent all day Saturday like that, and Ronda thoroughly enjoyed rubbing sunscreen all over Gayla's body.

"I do so love your body," she said.

"Thank you. Should I rub it on you?" Gayla asked.

"Nah. I got that."

"Okay, but don't miss any spots. I don't want you to be crispy. I've got plans for you tonight."

"I won't get burned. Believe me. I derive no pleasure from a sunburn."

"Fair enough. I trust you."

And with that, she went back into the water. Ronda really wished she could get out in the deeper water. It was the temperature of bath water. But she didn't want to risk her knee. So she was extremely cautious and Gayla was extremely paranoid, which combined to keep her out of water above her ankles.

And after a day on the beach, they went out for cocktails and dinner at a nice steakhouse. They watched the waves break along the beach as they enjoyed steak and lobster and margaritas. Ronda was relaxed and Gayla seemed to be enjoying herself as well.

"We need to do this more often," Ronda said.

"Well, considering we've only been a couple for a little while, it's not like we've had this opportunity before."

"True. But now that we are, we need to make an effort to spend more time at the beach. Maybe I'll buy a beach house here."

"That would be amazing," Gayla said.

"Yeah. I think I'm going to look into that. Or have you look into it for me."

"I'd love to. And if we can't get down here, we can always rent it out."

"You're a genius, baby. We'll have our own getaway and another source of income. I do like the way you think."

"So let's grab one of those newspapers that I saw on the way in. We'll look at properties tomorrow before we have to leave the island," Gayla said.

They went back to the condo. As soon as the door was closed, Ronda trapped Gayla against it.

"What are you doing?" Gayla said.

"This." Ronda kissed Gayla hard on the lips, not accepting anything less than a passionate kiss in return.

"I need you," Ronda whispered when the kiss ended. "I need you right now."

"Then take me, baby. I can't wait."

Ronda fumbled with Gayla's clothes as she struggled not to twist her knee.

"I'll be so glad when I'm one hundred percent," Ronda said. "Come on. Let's go to the bedroom. I'll undress you there."

Ronda sat on the bed and Gayla stood between her legs. Ronda finished unbuttoning Gayla's blouse and slipped it down her arms and off. Next, she unhooked her bra and tossed it on top of the blouse. She pulled Gayla closer and took a nipple in her mouth. She ran her tongue over it as she sucked it in.

"Mm," she said as she released the nipple. "You feel so fucking good."

"You're making me feel pretty good, too."

"Yeah? Well, let's see how good I can make you feel."

She unbuttoned Gayla's slacks and slowly lowered the zipper. She pushed them down over her hips and Gayla stepped out of them. Her panties were next. She stood naked in front of Ronda, who skimmed her body with her hands.

"You're so fucking gorgeous," Ronda said. "Just gorgeous. Sometimes I want you so bad I don't even know where to start."

"Is this one of those times?"

"It is."

Gayla took Ronda's hands and placed them on her breasts as she leaned in and kissed her. Ronda caressed and fondled the soft mounds as she got lost in the kiss. Her head grew light and she felt dizzy as the kiss intensified. She was so crazy about Gayla. Nothing else mattered.

"Come here. Lie down with me," she said.

Ronda scooted back on the bed and rolled over to look at Gayla lying next to her.

"Shouldn't we get your clothes off you?" Gayla said.

"Oh, yeah. I'm slightly overdressed."

Ronda got up and undressed as quickly as she could. Then she lay back down with Gayla. She dragged her arm up and down her body.

"You have the most amazing body," she said.

"It's not as firm as yours."

"Mine is muscular from working out. Yours is soft and sweet like a woman's should be."

"I rather like yours," Gayla said, pressing her hand against Ronda's hard stomach.

"I need to start lifting again. I'm going to get soft."

"Only do what your therapist and trainer say you can, baby. I don't want you hurting yourself."

"I won't. I've come so far."

Gayla rolled over on top of her. They were breast to breast. Ronda slid her hand between them and found Gayla wet and ready for her.

"You're so nice and warm," she said.

"I've been wanting this since this morning."

"Why didn't you say so?"

"I thought waiting would make it extra special."

"Well, it's going to be special. It always is with you," Ronda said.

She kissed her again while her fingers found Gayla's special spot.

"Oh, baby," Gayla broke the kiss. "Oh, my God, what you do to me."

"You like that, huh? That feels good?"

"Oh, yes. Please don't stop."

"I won't. I want you to come for me, babe," Ronda said.

"I'm going to. Oh, yes. Oh, God, yes."

"Come for me."

"Oh, *yes*, Ronda. Oh, yes. Oh, yes. Oh, my God."

"Yeah? We got it?" Ronda said.

"Oh, my God, yes, we got it."

"Mm. Good. Now come here and let me hold you."

"Not so fast, stud. Now it's my turn to get you."

"You sure you have it in you?"

"I'm positive," Gayla said.

She rolled off Ronda and bent to suckle at a nipple.

"I love how small and perfect your nipples are," she said. "They suit you."

She moved her hand down Ronda's body to where her legs met. She found her as wet as she felt.

"Mm. Someone's excited."

"Making love to you always excites me."

"Excellent answer."

Gayla stroked Ronda between her legs, playing first with her clit before entering her. She slid her fingers inside and moved them about, then pulled them out.

"More," Ronda said. "I need more."

Gayla added another finger and plunged them deep inside her. She pulled them out. She repeated it over and over until Ronda was so wet it was hard to keep her fingers inside her. She pulled them out and rubbed Ronda's swollen clit until Ronda issued a guttural moan indicating she had reached her climax.

"Wow. That was amazing," Ronda said.

"Yes, it was. I love pleasing you."

"You do a damned fine job of it. You ready for some sleep now?"

"Sure." She snuggled against Ronda and they both fell asleep.

The next morning, they went out for breakfast and, over breakfast, perused beach houses for sale.

"You know," Ronda said. "It doesn't even have to be right on the water. I would be okay if it wasn't."

"Settle down. Let's see what's out there first."

There were several pages of listings.

"We don't have a clue where any of these are," Ronda said. "We're going to have to drive all over the island to find them."

"What else are we doing today?"

"I suppose that's true. So let's start choosing. This one looks nice." She pointed to a picture on the second page.

Gayla took a pen out of her purse and circled it.

"What else?"

They spent a half an hour going through the pictures, choosing which houses looked nice and which ones were close to the water and which ones were not even worth considering. Their top choice was large, spacious, and having an open house that day. Ronda could hardly contain her excitement. She'd been thinking of investing in property for quite a while. What better to invest in than a beach house?

It wasn't easy for Ronda to navigate up all the stairs to get to the actual house, but she understood the stairs were necessary. The houses were all built on pilings in case of hurricanes. So she managed to get to the top with Gayla's help. They toured the house and, at the end of it, Ronda was in love.

"Shouldn't we go look at other places, too?" Gayla said.

"No. I like this place. Why climb a million stairs when I know there's no place I'll like as much as this one?"

"Okay. If you're sure."

Ronda found the agent and told her she was representing herself and would like to make an offer on the house. She offered five thousand more than the asking price, just in case. Gayla stood by her as the Realtor and Ronda talked. When they were through, Ronda carefully made her way down the stairs.

"Man, those stairs were not made for bad knees. I might put in an outdoor elevator."

"What?"

"You know. Like a bucket to lift me from the ground to the deck."

"Do you want that expense when the injury is only temporary?" Gayla said.

"I don't like coming down those steep stairs with my knee. It was scary. I'll get the elevator thingy. I saw one at another house, so I know they do them out here. It'll be much safer for me."

"Well, you're assuming you're going to get the house."

"I am," Ronda said. "I can feel it in my bones."

They went back to the condo, packed up their things, and headed back to the city. The following morning, Ronda had physical therapy. Gayla drove her to her appointment and sat at the far end of the gym reading while Ronda went through her exercises.

"So, hey, I think I hurt my knee this weekend." Ronda glanced over at Gayla who seemed engrossed in her book.

"How so?"

"I got a little too far out in the waves."

"Oh, shit. I hope you didn't undo any progress that's been done."

"I don't know. It still feels stronger. It just hurts like a mother fucker," Ronda said.

"I bet. Well, it's for sure we won't start weaning you off the pills yet."

"Thanks. They really help."

"You really need to be more careful, Meyers. I don't tell you things for my health. I tell you them for yours."

When they finished their exercises, the therapist went in to the team doctor's office and came out with a new prescription for Vicodin for Ronda.

"Take care of yourself. Keep up with your home exercises and try not to hurt yourself again before I see you on Friday."

"See you then," Ronda said. She walked over to Gayla who put her book in her purse and stood.

"Ready?" Ronda said.

"Sure."

The ride home felt icy cool to Ronda. She felt like Gayla was pissed at her, but she had no idea why.

"Everything okay?" she asked when they got home.

"No," Gayla said. She spun around in the front room and glared at Ronda. "You have a problem and you need to deal with it."

"I don't have a problem." Ronda felt a rock begin to form in the pit of her stomach. "What the hell are you talking about?"

"You and those pills. I've been concerned about them for a long time, but now I know for sure. You are addicted to your pain pills."

"You've got a lot of nerve. When was the last time you had your knee blown out in a football game?"

"Very funny. That's not the point."

"That's the point exactly. You have no idea what you're talking about."

"Ronda, you told your therapist you got too far out in the waves."

"So?"

"So we were extra careful to make sure you didn't. I know it was a lie to get more pills."

"So I needed more pills and wasn't sure they'd give them to me. So I told a little white lie. Where's the harm?"

"The harm is that you're addicted to those things," Gayla said.

"Bullshit. I need them for the pain."

"You don't. Not anymore. Sure you did in the beginning. But you're past that. Everyone says the pain should be gone and I think it is. I think you're addicted to Vicodin. I've been in pain, too, you know. Remember my brother? I've needed you to be strong for me recently and all you've cared about are those damned pills."

"Well, you're wrong about the addiction. And you should have said something if you were feeling sad about Jesse."

"I shouldn't have to. You should have noticed my mood. You should have cared enough to ask how I was feeling. But you didn't. The only thing important to you is Vicodin."

"That is so not true. And I'm not a mind reader."

"Whatever. I'm not going to stay here and watch you be hooked on some substance," Gayla said.

"What the hell is that supposed to mean?"

"It means I'm out of here."

Ronda felt the panic in her gut. She couldn't lose Gayla. But she wasn't going to give up her pills. She needed to figure out a way to keep Gayla there.

"Babe, please don't go. I need you. We belong together. Without you, there is no me."

"Maybe you do need me, but it seems to me you need those pills more. Call me when you're off them."

And with that, Gayla stormed out the door.

Ronda hobbled to the couch and sat down. She put her left leg up and leaned back.

"Shit," she said out loud. How could Gayla have left her? How long would she stay gone?

Ronda got back up and poured herself a scotch and took four Vicodin. That should ease the pain in her heart, she thought. She sat back on the couch and turned on the television. Nothing caught her eye as she flipped through the channels. She turned it off and sat there as darkness settled in. She ordered a pizza, but wasn't hungry when it got there. Her house was so empty without Gayla. She needed to get her back. But how? She wasn't ready to give up her pain pills yet. She just needed Gayla to see she wasn't hooked on them. That should be easy enough to do. Right?

Chapter Twenty

Ronda woke the following morning to the ringing of her telephone. She knew the caller by the ringtone. It was Gayla.

"Hello?" Ronda said.

"Hello." The voice on the other end was cool and distant. "I figured that just because you and I are no longer an item, that didn't mean I couldn't still work for you. Do you agree with that?"

Ronda's heart leapt in her chest. She would still get to see Gayla. She was shaking she was so excited. She told herself to be cool.

"I totally agree with that," she said.

"Good. I've set you up with two houses to show today. We'll do them just like we used to. I'll brief you then leave to go to the next house."

"That won't work, Gayla. I'll need you to stay and show the second story."

"How long are you going to need that knee brace?"

"Not much longer. I'm sure we'll get rid of it soon. I'm just not quite ready yet."

"Just like you're not quite ready to get off the pain pills," Gayla said.

"Don't start with me. You don't know the pain I'm in."

"I don't think you're in pain. I think maybe it's in your head. Or maybe you just like the way they make your feel."

"That's enough of this conversation," Ronda said. "Just tell me where to be and when."

Gayla gave Ronda the address of the first house.

"I'll see you there at one," Gayla said.

"I'll be there."

Ronda hung up. She wanted to throw her phone across the room. Gayla was being such a bitch. Ronda wanted her back, but didn't want her making all her crazy accusations. So, Ronda took pain pills. There was nothing wrong with that. They were prescribed by doctors, so they must be needed, right? Her doctors wouldn't prescribe them if she didn't need them.

She hobbled to the bathroom without them and took her shower. She dried off and got back to her bedroom. Success, she thought. Baby steps. She dressed in a white suit with a light blue shirt. She looked appropriate for Houston in the summer.

Driving felt weird to her, simply because she hadn't done it in so long. But it was just like riding a bike and soon she felt at ease behind the wheel. She listened to Siri and arrived at the house even before Gayla. She had butterflies in her stomach. She was so nervous about seeing Gayla. It still hadn't really soaked in that they were kaput.

She sat in her car with the air conditioner running until she saw Gayla pull up. She got out of her car and went over to Gayla and had to fight the urge to kiss her, but Gayla was all business.

"Let's get inside so we can go over the finer details of this sale."

They went in and found the dining room. They leaned at the bar and went over what points of the house Ronda should emphasize and what points she should glaze over. She had it down just as the doorbell rang.

"I'll be here," Gayla said. "Only if they need to go upstairs."

"I understand." Ronda went to the door and opened it to find her potential buyers. She showed the house just as she and Gayla had discussed and ended up with the couple making an offer. One down, one to go.

When the couple was gone, she went over to hug Gayla.

"We did it," she said.

"It would probably be better if you didn't hug me," Gayla said.

"Ah, come on. What's the harm?"

"I'd rather a drug addict not touch me. That's all."

"Ouch," Ronda said.

"Well, I call a spade a spade."

"Okay. I don't want to talk about this right now. Where's the next house?"

"Of course you don't. You just let me know when you do." She gave Ronda the next address and they took off.

Ronda pulled in right before Gayla. She popped four Vicodin and took a swig of water. She was ready to deal with Gayla and her negative attitude.

The second house went well, but the potential buyers left without making an offer. Ronda was bummed. Not that she needed a sale every time, though that would be wonderful, but she really thought she had the couple convinced.

"I wonder what went wrong with that," she said.

"I don't know. I thought they were for sure going to make an offer."

"Oh, well. So no drinks for you tonight?"

"Not with you. We're not together anymore, remember?"

"We used to go out for drinks before we were an item. Remember that?" Ronda said.

"Well, if it's all the same to you, I'd rather not. Thanks. I'll see you tomorrow."

Ronda watched as Gayla drove off.

"Shit," she said. She was lonely and missed Gayla and the times they'd had together. She wanted Gayla back. She needed to figure out how to get her back.

The rest of the week was more of the same. They sold three more houses. Ronda was feeling good. Gayla seemed to be happy with the work they were doing, but when it was time to wrap up the day, she grew aloof.

Ronda was almost ready to beg for Gayla to come home by the time Thursday was over. But she didn't. She knew what the answer would be and her pride had been damaged too much as it was.

Friday at physical therapy, Ronda broached the subject of getting out of her knee brace.

"I encourage it. You've had it on much longer than most people, but with all the pain you've been in, we've been hesitant to push you too hard. Your leg should be strong enough to support you now with no problem. But since you've been relying on the brace, be careful. Don't do anything crazy."

"I'm mostly concerned with going up and down stairs."

"Your knee should support you with all the exercises we've been doing. But I would say be careful. Hold the handrail. Don't put yourself in a position to get hurt."

"Okay. Thanks."

"How's your pain doing?"

"It's okay. I still hurt. But I have plenty of meds for now," Ronda said.

"How bad is the pain, though? We were thinking about doing an MRI to see if you did any damage to it in the Gulf."

"No. I'm pretty sure I didn't. I mean, it hurts, but it always has."

"That doesn't make any sense."

"No?" Ronda asked. "Why not?"

"Because you're a fine specimen of physicality. You were in great shape when you got hurt and you're doing your exercises and I see improvement every time I see you. So, the pain should be gone by now."

"I don't know what to tell you," Ronda said. "It still hurts."

She left her therapy appointment determined to spend her weekend getting out of the brace. She got home and felt depressed. She missed having Gayla there with her, to talk to, to just hang with. She walked to the kitchen, took some pain pills, and poured herself a scotch. She walked to the living room and sat down. So far, so good without the brace.

She wanted to call Gayla, but didn't have a reason to. She just missed her. She wanted to be with her. It was more than just the sex, though that was great and she definitely missed that, but there was so much more. They were good friends and could talk about anything together.

Ronda turned on the television and soon drifted off to a soccer game. She awoke in the middle of the night, alone and confused. She soon realized where she was and who wasn't with her. Depressed, she made it to her room and passed out on her bed.

She got up in the morning and made herself a bagel and coffee. She took her pain pills, four of them, and sat at the dining room table to read the paper. That's when her phone rang. It was Gayla.

"Hey," Ronda said.

"Hey yourself. How are you feeling?"

"I feel great."

"I'm sure you do. When did you take your pain pills?"

"I'm not going to discuss my pills with you," Ronda said.

"Of course not. I'm just calling to let you know our schedule for the week."

"You've already got us set up?"

"Yes. It's easy to only do two a day, three days a week. Now, do you have a pen and paper?"

"Got it. Shoot."

Gayla gave Ronda the details of the houses and then tried to hang up.

"Can we do lunch today?" Ronda said.

"No."

"Please? I promise to be sober. I miss you, Gayla."

"I'd be lying if I said I didn't miss you, too, Ronda, but you have a problem and I can't sit by and let you do this to yourself. Especially because it could really hurt your career. I just can't be party to that."

"I'm not going to hurt my career," Ronda stated emphatically. "I'm under control. You need to get over it. Never mind. Forget I said anything about lunch."

"No. I'd like to see you. You know, I miss you, too, Ronda."

They decided where to meet and when. Ronda checked her watch. She had five hours. No worry. She soaked in the hot tub for a while, took her shower, got dressed and took some more pain pills. She still had an hour to go. She sat on the couch to watch some golf to pass the time.

She woke to the sound of her phone ringing. It was Gayla.

"Where are you?" She said.

"I'm sorry. I fell asleep. I'll be right there."

"No. Don't bother. I'll see you Tuesday."

The line went dead. Ronda stood holding her phone.

"Shit!" she said. "Shit, shit, shit."

She got up and grabbed a beer from the refrigerator.

How could she have fallen asleep like that? Golf was boring to watch, but still... She'd blown a chance to see Gayla. She was agitated. She checked her watch. She wasn't supposed to take her pills for another two hours. But she needed something to calm her nerves. She took two of them and downed them with a swig of beer. That should help, she thought.

She went back to the couch. Damn, she wanted to see Gayla. She called her back.

"Hello?"

"Look, I'm sorry I crashed. I was watching golf. What can I say? Can we do dinner?"

"No. I think you probably passed out, and now I don't want to see you again. So no dinner and I'll see you Tuesday."

"But—"

"No buts. You need to get it together, Ronda. You've already lost me. Do you want to lose your careers, too? I am watching you closely when you show houses. If I see any signs that you're not on top of your game, I will quit working for you. I want you to know that."

"No. That's not fair. Everyone makes mistakes. If I'm not on top of my game one day, it's not fair that you'd quit."

"We'll see, Ronda. That's my intention anyway."

"I promise I won't disappoint you, Gayla," Ronda said.

"I sure hope not."

The call ended and Ronda felt fear in the pit of her stomach. She couldn't lose Gayla forever. Not now that she'd found her. And if she lost her professionally, she'd really be screwed. She needed to keep things together. Maybe it was time to get off the pills. But could she?

Ronda went into her office and searched the Internet for ways to make herself quit taking the Vicodin. Her greatest fear was that the pain would come back. She told herself if that happened, she could start taking them again, but only two at a time, every four to six hours as instructed. Not four at a time every three to four hours as she felt like it.

One of the recommendations was to go to a doctor and get a substitute for the pills. That didn't sound good to her. She didn't want to trade one pill for another. Besides, she couldn't let the doctors know she was getting prescriptions from both of them. They'd never trust her again. And if she came clean with the team doctor, she might not play again. So, no. Talking to a doctor was off the table. She was going to have to do this on her own.

The first thing they recommended was to start weaning herself off the drugs. Not stopping all at once. She checked her bottles and decided she had enough to do this. She had two almost full bottles. She should be able to work herself off the Vicodin. The stress of not taking them anymore caused her to pour three in her hand, but she put them back in the bottle. No. She was going to take them as often as they were prescribed, not whenever she felt stressed. It wouldn't be easy, but if this is what it took to get Gayla back, then this is what she was going to do.

She already felt tense and uneasy. She had to find something to do. She went out to the hot tub and relaxed. It felt good to just let herself be at peace. When she got out of the tub, she checked her watch. Still not time for pills? Damn. This was going to be harder than she thought. She drove down to a local burger joint to try to take her mind off of it. She had a burger, fries and a couple of beers. It was good. It only took an hour. That was bad.

With nothing else to do, she drove back to her house. It was still early but she thought about going to bed for lack of anything else to do at home. She put on a DVD and sat back with a beer to watch it. The movie ended and she decided to go to bed. At that point, she was allowed to take two pills, which she did. She went to bed.

Sleep escaped Ronda, though. She tried to get comfortable, but couldn't. She had her air conditioner set to sixty-eight, yet still she was burning up. She tossed and turned, and finally dozed about six in the morning.

She got up around ten and felt like dogmeat. Her head hurt, her stomach was doing somersaults, and she was exhausted. She made herself breakfast and took two pills. They did nothing to relieve any of the symptoms. She was afraid her breakfast was not going to stay down. She curled up on her bed and willed herself to feel better. She finally fell asleep.

CHAPTER TWENTY-ONE

Ronda woke to the late afternoon sun shining its rays through her curtains. She checked her watch. It was five thirty. Thank God she'd slept so much of the day away. She felt a little better, so she got up and started making dinner. The smell of it made her nauseous. She told herself to power through it, but it was no use. She hobbled to the bathroom and threw up.

She threw the partially made meal away and made herself two slices of toast. She drank a big glass of water and took two more pills. Maybe stopping taking the pills wasn't such a great idea, she thought. But then she thought of Gayla and knew it would be worth it.

She still felt queasy, so didn't trust her stomach to eat anything else. She made her way to the couch. She was proud of herself that she hadn't used her brace so far that weekend. Her knee really was strong. If only it didn't hurt. But then, everything hurt. She felt like her body was cramping up. She went back out to the hot tub to try to ease some of the muscle aches. It felt good, but her stomach was starting to act up again.

"Shit," she said. She'd finally accepted it was going to be an unpleasant process.

She went back in, threw up again, and lay back down on the bed. Sleep escaped her again as she tossed and turned all night. She was exhausted when she finally fell asleep after looking at the clock one last time and seeing seven.

Her alarm went off at ten. She had physical therapy at eleven. She felt like something the dog dragged in. She climbed into her truck and drove to the practice facilities.

"Holy shit, Meyers. You look like crap. You feeling okay?"

"Yeah," Ronda lied. "I've just got a touch of some bug or something."

"We could have put this off another day."

"No. I want to stick with my schedule."

"Okay, then. Let's get started. You just let me know if I'm pushing you too hard or if you need to quit."

"Okay."

"Man, you really look green around the gills," her therapist said.

"Yeah, well, if I'm going to get sick, I know where the bathroom is," Ronda said.

"Talk about dedication. I'm impressed."

"I've got to get stronger. Come on. Let's do this."

The therapist went easier on Ronda than usual because she was weaker than normal. They did their exercises and she sent Ronda on her way with some new home exercises to do.

"Take care of yourself," she said. "I'd like to see you feeling better by Friday."

Friday, Ronda thought. Would she feel better? How long would these withdrawals go on? And was she strong enough to withstand them? She drove home, ordered a pizza, and sat in front of the television. There was nothing good on. Agitated, she got up and paced the room. She needed her pills. She checked her watch. One hour until she got to take two. She would be able to take them as soon as she ate her pizza.

The pizza arrived. She ate and took two pills. She shivered. Her whole body felt like one giant cramp. She went out to the hot tub again to try to relax some. It worked. Her muscles unwound while she soaked. But, just as the previous night, her stomach began to object to the pizza.

"Why did I even try?" she said to herself. She climbed out of the tub and lost her lunch. She lay on her bed in a fetal position and fought the tears that threatened. She wondered briefly if she should call Gayla. Gayla would be able to come over and make her feel better. But no, Gayla couldn't know she was withdrawing. But Ronda had serious doubts about keeping it together while showing houses the rest of the week. She could call Gayla and claim she had the flu, but she needed to keep busy. She couldn't just sit around the house and feel like shit all day. It was a lesser of two evils. She would do her damnedest to show houses.

The week did not go well for Ronda. She arrived at the first house the next day and Gayla was immediately concerned.

"You look like shit. What's going on?"

"I've got a touch of the flu," Ronda lied. "I should be fine. Now tell me about the buyers and about the house."

Gayla gave Ronda a brief overview, making sure, as usual, to point out the top selling points and what to skim past.

Ronda nodded her understanding as she stood in the kitchen, concentrating on nothing but keeping her stomach down. It was no use.

"Where's the restroom?" she said.

Gayla pointed down the hall and Ronda hurried to throw up. She brushed her teeth with the toothbrush and toothpaste she had brought for just this reason and walked back out to see Gayla standing there.

"Are you sure you're okay?"

"Yeah. I mean, I'm sick, but I'll survive."

Just then the couple walked up, precluding any further conversation. Gayla drove off to the next house while Ronda did her best to sell the one she was at. She got the couple to make an offer. She was beyond excited. The couple left and Ronda went back to hug the toilet again.

The rest of the week passed with a fifty-fifty ratio of offers. That was wonderful, and both Ronda and Gayla were happy about them.

"You sure seem to be feeling better," Gayla said after they'd shown their last house on Thursday.

"I am." Ronda was still taking her pills, but the flu-like symptoms had subsided. She figured the worst was over.

"I was really worried about you. You looked horrible yesterday and the day before."

"Yeah. The flu hit me hard. I'm not out of the woods yet, but I'm definitely feeling better."

"Well, good. You have a nice, restful weekend and I'll call you when I've got our appointments for next week set up," Gayla said.

"Sounds good."

Ronda drove home. She checked her watch. Twenty minutes until pain pill time. She wondered what would happen if she didn't take them. She made up her mind to find out. She had cut down to two pills every six hours. If she skipped a dose successfully, she would be one step closer to ending her addiction.

So she did it. She did not take her pills. She felt a little queasy, but it was nothing like it had been coming off the four pills whenever she felt like taking them. She was exhausted and climbed into bed and slept.

Friday, her therapist was impressed at how much better she looked. She pushed Ronda hard, but Ronda kept up with her.

"You know, Meyers, you're doing a great job. You've been so dedicated this whole time, but today something seems different. It's like you're even more determined. I appreciate it. You've come a long way."

"Thanks. It's taken a while, but I think I can see light at the end of the tunnel."

"Sure you can. It's there."

"I just want to make sure I'm a hundred and ten percent for next year. I need to start," Ronda said.

"Don't you worry. We'll have you in tip-top shape by then."

"I'm counting on it."

"All right, Meyers. Enjoy your weekend and I'll see you Monday."

"Sounds good. See you then."

Ronda drove home feeling better than she had since she'd had her knee blown out. And she had continued to skip doses of her meds. She figured by the end of the weekend, she'd be off the pills altogether. And then she'd be able to tell Gayla and they'd get back together. Ronda was walking on air when she got back to her house.

And that was when it got hard. She was alone and bored and knew that the pills would make her feel better. She had to do something to get her mind off the pills. She called Gayla.

"Hello?" Gayla said.

"Hey. It's me. I wondered if you might be interested in getting some lunch or something."

"I don't know, Ronda…"

"Okay, well, if you won't do that, will you at least come over? I have a favor to ask of you."

"Again, I'm not sure that's such a good idea."

"It's important. Please."

"Fine. I'll be right over."

Ronda sat on the couch with her hands clasped tightly in her lap. She didn't want to think about the pills. She didn't want to take them, but didn't know if she was strong enough not to. She got up and walked out to the pool. She sat on one of her chairs out there, but the pull was still strong.

Damn it! What was taking Gayla so long? She got up and paced around the pool. She was so tempted to go into the house. But she'd been doing so well. At the moment, she was bored and irritated and she knew what she'd been doing to ease those feelings for over ten weeks now. She couldn't do it anymore. But if Gayla didn't get there soon, she might not be strong enough to hold out.

She heard her doorbell ring. Thank God, she thought. She answered it and saw Gayla standing there.

"Thank God you came." Ronda pulled her into a tight hug.

"Ronda, I don't think that's appropriate."

"But I needed you so bad. What took you so long?"

"Nothing. I got here as soon as I could. Now, would you please tell me what's going on?"

"Please. Come in. I have a huge favor to ask of you."

"That's what you said on the phone. What's this big favor?"

"Do you remember earlier this week when I had the flu?"

"Sure."

"It wasn't the flu, Gayla. I was coming off my pills."

"So you *did* have a problem?" Gayla said. "It's nice to hear you admit that."

"But here's where I need your help. I've gotten over the withdrawal symptoms. I'm pretty much over the pills."

"Great."

"Yeah, but not completely. I'm feeling antsy and bored and I'm afraid I'm going to take some."

"Okay. So, how can I help?"

"I can't even look at the pills right now, Gayla. I don't trust myself."

"I understand," Gayla said.

"So, I'm going to ask you to go into the kitchen first. The pills are on the counter."

Gayla walked over to the kitchen, put the pills in her purse, and walked back.

"Okay. Now what?"

"In the medicine chest in the bathroom. There's another bottle. Go get them, please. And then flush both bottles down the toilet."

Gayla left and returned.

"Did you find them?"

"I did."

"I didn't hear a flush," Ronda said.

"That's bad for the environment. I'll take them back to the doctors."

"Are you sure?"

"I'm sure."

"Just don't let me have them."

"I won't," Gayla said. "Now, let's go to lunch to get your mind off things."

"That would be great. Thank you. I really appreciate this."

"No problem, Ronda. I'm so proud of you for getting yourself off those things. Anything I can do to help, I'm all over."

They went out for a nice lunch. Gayla drove, so Ronda had a few beers. She was feeling much better by the time they were heading home.

"Thanks again," Ronda said. "I don't know if I would have been strong enough to get through this afternoon without you."

"You have to know that deep down, I'd never let you flounder. I'll always be there for you if you truly need me."

"I'm always going to need you, Gayla. I mean that. This whole week. What I've been through. It just about killed me to go through it alone. But I didn't want to admit to you that I'd been abusing the drugs, that I was addicted."

"I already knew that, though."

"I didn't want to let you know you were right. Call it pride."

"You never need to be prideful with me, Ronda."

"I see that now. I'm sorry," Ronda said.

"It's okay. Will you be okay now? Or do you want me to stay for a while?"

"I'd love it if you stayed. But if you can't, I'll understand."

"How about this? How about if I go return those medications now and then come back? I don't want them here with us. I think it would be too great a temptation for you."

"I agree. Go ahead and do what you need to and I'll be here waiting for you when you get back." She climbed out of the car and let herself into the house.

Ronda sat on the couch feeling better than she had in weeks. The foggy high she felt on the pills was gone. The withdrawals she'd felt coming off the pills was gone. She felt normal again. It was a wonderful sensation. And Gayla was coming back over. Life was good again. She was strong and happy.

Gayla arrived back at the house less than an hour later.

"That didn't take long," Ronda said.

"Nope. Easy peasy."

"Great. Thanks again for doing that for me."

"Anytime."

"So, what would you like to do now?" Ronda said.

"I don't know. I guess just hang."

"Did you want to swim or hit the hot tub?"

"I don't have my suit."

Ronda swallowed hard. She wanted to claim Gayla again. She wanted Gayla to be hers and hers alone. But was it too soon? How would Gayla feel?

"Do you need one?" Ronda said.

"Oh, Ronda. I don't know. It seems so soon. Like things are happening too fast."

"I understand. I had to ask. I do hope we'll be able to get back together now that I'm clean."

"Yes. I missed you something terrible."

"Yeah? I missed you, too. But I won't push you. You take your time deciding when it's right."

"Oh, screw it," Gayla said. "A nice swim would feel good. Can you swim?"

"I can get in the water."

"Well, that's a start."

"Nah. Seriously, I can swim some. I've done some aqua therapy with my therapist."

"Great. Well, let's hit the water."

"Okay. The robes are in my closet. You know where to find one."

"I'll be right out," Gayla said.

Ronda sat on the couch, a new form of unease creeping over her. She was nervous about Gayla. She forced herself to stay on the couch and not go watch her undress. Soon, she would be naked and it would be up to Gayla to set the pace of the afternoon. Ronda again thought that she didn't want to push things too fast. But damn, now that Gayla was there, she wanted her so fucking bad.

Gayla emerged from the bedroom dressed in a white fuzzy robe.

"You look great," Ronda said and kissed her on the cheek.

"Thanks." Gayla blushed.

"I'll go change now and meet you out there?"

"Sounds good."

Ronda quickly stripped and put on a robe. She was out back in a flash.

"You ready to do this?" she asked nervously.

"Sure. It's not like we haven't seen each other naked before."

"Very true."

Ronda dropped her robe on a lounge and used the steps to descend into the water. She purposefully didn't turn around until she heard Gayla in the water behind her. She turned and caught the sight of her naked body and her clit swelled.

Gayla approached her slowly, purposefully.

"You look amazing, Ronda."

"Thanks. So do you."

Gayla rested her hands on Ronda's shoulders before moving them down to her chest.

"I've missed this body."

Ronda swallowed hard.

"I've missed yours."

"Kiss me, Ronda."

Ronda lowered her lips and kissed Gayla softly on her mouth.

"Mm," Gayla said. "That was nice."

Ronda walked over to the side of the pool. Gayla followed her.

"Is everything all right?" Gayla said.

"Yeah. I just don't want my legs giving out from kissing you in the middle of the pool. I feel safer here at the edge."

"Is your knee giving you troubles?"

"It's not my knee at all," Ronda said. "It's my body responding to yours."

She dragged her hand down Gayla's arm.

"You're so beautiful," she said.

"Thank you. Will you kiss me again?"

"Heck yeah."

Ronda kissed her again, harder than before. She pried open Gayla's lips and moved her tongue into her mouth where it danced with Gayla's. They kissed for several minutes until Ronda pulled away, breathless.

"I need you, babe. I've got to have you. Please."

"Let's go inside," Gayla said.

"Oh, yeah."

They quickly dried off and Ronda took Gayla's hand and sat on the bed with her. She kissed her softly at first, then with more need as the kiss intensified. They fell back on the bed, their hands roving over each other's bodies as they kissed.

Ronda cupped Gayla's breasts with her hands and Gayla moaned in her mouth. Ronda was going mad with desire. She kissed down Gayla's neck and chest until her mouth replaced her hand on a breast. She sucked all over the mound before finally taking her nipple in her mouth.

Gayla groaned.

"Oh, my God, you make me feel so good," she said.

"Mm," was all Ronda could say with her mouth full.

She continued to suck and roll the nub around on her tongue. She was dizzy with the need to please Gayla. She released her nipple from her mouth and played with it with her fingers. She kissed lower down Gayla's body until she was between her legs.

"My God, you're beautiful," she said. She had missed the sight and smell and taste that were all Gayla. Her uniqueness made Ronda even wetter than she already was. She licked along Gayla before she dipped her tongue inside her. She licked as deep as she could go and was rewarded with Gayla gyrating on the bed, urging her deeper. She moved her mouth to Gayla's clit and sucked it into her mouth. She ran her tongue around it and flicked the tip of it and Gayla crushed Ronda's head with her legs as she cried out.

She kissed her way back up until she could kiss Gayla on her mouth. She kissed her as hard as she could. She kissed her with every ounce of need she was feeling.

Gayla rolled Ronda over on to her back. She kissed down her body until she could take a nipple in her mouth. She sucked and played with Ronda's nipple as she slid her hand down to where her legs met. Ronda knew she was wet. And Gayla playing with her nipple just made her wetter.

"Look at this. Someone is ready for me."

"Dear God. Please take me," Ronda said.

Ronda spread her legs and arched her back as Gayla slipped her fingers inside her. Over and over, she plunged them, deeper and deeper with each thrust.

"Oh, yeah. That's it," Ronda said.

Gayla took her thumb and rubbed it along Ronda's clit, and that was all it took to shoot Ronda into orbit. She came back to reality in a thick, pleasant fog.

"Oh, babe. You are the best," she said.

"Thanks, baby. I think you're pretty darned good, too."

"Thanks."

Gayla moved up and snuggled in Ronda's arms.

"So, babe?" Ronda said.

"Yeah?"

"What do you think? I could have some teammates at your house this weekend and we can move you over here."

"I can't think of anything I'd rather do this weekend."

Ronda kissed the top of her head.

"Neither can I, babe. Neither can I."

About the Author

MJ Williamz was raised on California's central coast, which she left at age seventeen to pursue an education. She graduated from Chico State and it was in Chico that she rediscovered her love of writing. It wasn't until she moved to Portland, however, that her writing really took off, with the publication of her first short story in 2003.

MJ is the author of fourteen books, including three Goldie Award winners. She has also had over thirty short stories published, most of them erotica with a few romances and a few horrors thrown in for good measure. She lives in Houston with her wife, fellow author Laydin Michaels, and their fur babies. You can reach her at mjwilliamz@aol.com

Books Available from Bold Strokes Books

A Country Girl's Heart by Dena Blake. When Kat Jackson gets a second chance at love, following her heart will prove the hardest decision of all. (978-1-63555-134-1)

Dangerous Waters by Radclyffe. Life, death, and war on the home front. Two women join forces against a powerful opponent, nature itself. (978-1-63555-233-1)

Fury's Death by Brey Willows. When all we hold sacred fails, who will be there to save us? (978-1-63555-063-4)

It's Not a Date by Heather Blackmore. Kade's desire to keep things with Jen on a professional level is in Jen's best interest. Yet what's in Kade's best interest...is Jen. (978-1-63555-149-5)

Killer Winter by Kay Bigelow. Just when she thought things could get no worse, homicide Lieutenant Leah Samuels learns the woman she loves has betrayed her in devastating ways. (978-1-63555-177-8)

Score by MJ Williamz. Will an addiction to pain pills destroy Ronda's chance with the woman she loves or will she come out on top and score a happily ever after? (978-1-62639-807-8)

Spring's Wake by Aurora Rey. When wanderer Willa Lange falls for Provincetown B&B owner Nora Calhoun, will past hurts and a fifteen-year age gap keep them from finding love? (978-1-63555-035-1)

The Lurid Sea by Tom Cardamone. Cursed to spend eternity on his knees, Nerites is having the time of his life. (978-1-62639-911-2)

The Northwoods by Jane Hoppen. When Evelyn Bauer, disguised as her dead husband, George, travels to a Northwoods logging camp to work, she and the camp cook Sarah Bell forge a friendship fraught with both tenderness and turmoil. (978-1-63555-143-3)

Truth or Dare by C. Spencer. For a group of six lesbian friends, life changes course after one long snow-filled weekend. (978-1-63555-148-8)

A Heart to Call Home by Jeannie Levig. When Jessie Weldon returns to her hometown after thirty years, can she and her childhood crush Dakota Scott heal the tragic past that links them? (978-1-63555-059-7)

Children of the Healer by Barbara Ann Wright. Life becomes desperate for ex-soldier Cordelia Ross when the indigenous aliens of her planet are drawn into a civil war and old enemies linger in the shadows. Book Three of the Godfall Series. (978-1-63555-031-3)

Hearts Like Hers by Melissa Brayden. Coffee shop owner Autumn Primm is ready to cut loose and live a little, but is the baggage that comes with out-of-towner Kate Carpenter too heavy for anything long term? (978-1-63555-014-6)

Love at Cooper's Creek by Missouri Vaun. Shaw Daily flees corporate life to find solace in the rural Blue Ridge Mountains, but escapism eludes her when her attentions are captured by small town beauty Kate Elkins. (978-1-62639-960-0)

Somewhere Over Lorain Road by Bud Gundy. Over forty years after murder allegations shattered the Esker family, can Don Esker find the true killer and clear his dying father's name? (978-1-63555-124-2)

Twice in a Lifetime by PJ Trebelhorn. Detective Callie Burke can't deny the growing attraction to her late friend's widow, Taylor Fletcher, who also happens to own the bar where Callie's sister works. (978-1-63555-033-7)

Undiscovered Affinity by Jane Hardee. Will a no strings attached affair be enough to break Olivia's control and convince Cardic that love does exist? (978-1-63555-061-0)

Between Sand and Stardust by Tina Michele. Are the lifelong bonds of love strong enough to conquer time, distance, and heartache when Haven Thorne and Willa Bennette are given another chance at forever? (978-1-62639-940-2)

Charming the Vicar by Jenny Frame. When magician and atheist Finn Kane seeks refuge in an English village after a spiritual crisis, can local vicar Bridget Claremont restore her faith in life and love? (978-1-63555-029-0)

Data Capture by Jesse J. Thoma. Lola Walker is undercover on the hunt for cybercriminals while trying not to notice the woman who might be perfectly wrong for her for all the right reasons. (978-1-62639-985-3)

Epicurean Delights by Renee Roman. Ariana Marks had no idea a leisure swim would lead to being rescued, in more ways than one, by the charismatic Hudson Frost. (978-1-63555-100-6)

Heart of the Devil by Ali Vali. We know most of Cain and Emma Casey's story, but *Heart of the Devil* will take you back to where it began one fateful night with a tray loaded with beer. (978-1-63555-045-0)

Known Threat by Kara A. McLeod. When Special Agent Ryan O'Connor reluctantly questions who protects the Secret Service, she learns courage truly is found in unlikely places. Agent O'Connor Series #3. (978-1-63555-132-7)

Seer and the Shield by D. Jackson Leigh. Time is running out for the Dragon Horse Army while two unlikely heroines struggle to put aside their attraction and find a way to stop a deadly cult. Dragon Horse War, Book 3. (978-1-63555-170-9)

Sinister Justice by Steve Pickens. When a vigilante targets citizens of Jake Finnigan's hometown, Jake and his partner Sam fall under suspicion themselves as they investigate the murders. (978-1-63555-094-8)

The Universe Between Us by Jane C. Esther. Ana Mitchell must make the hardest choice of her life: the promise of new love Jolie Dann on Earth, or a humanity-saving mission to colonize Mars. (978-1-63555-106-8)

Touch by Kris Bryant. Can one touch heal a heart? (978-1-63555-084-9)

Change in Time by Robyn Nyx. Working in the past is hell on your future. The Extractor Series: Book Two. (978-1-62639-880-1)

Love After Hours by Radclyffe. When Gina Antonelli agrees to renovate Carrie Longmire's new house, she doesn't welcome Carrie's overtures at friendship or her own unexpected attraction. A Rivers Community Novel. (978-1-63555-090-0)

Nantucket Rose by CF Frizzell. Maggie Jordan can't wait to convert an historic Nantucket home into a B&B, but doesn't expect to fall for mariner Ellis Chilton, who has more claim to the house than Maggie realizes. (978-1-63555-056-6)

Picture Perfect by Lisa Moreau. Falling in love wasn't supposed to be part of the stakes for Olive and Gabby, rival photographers in the competition of a lifetime. (978-1-62639-975-4)

Set the Stage by Karis Walsh. Actress Emilie Danvers takes the stage again in Ashland, Oregon, little realizing that landscaper Arden Philips is about to offer her a very personal romantic lead role. (978-1-63555-087-0)

Strike a Match by Fiona Riley. When their attempts at matchmaking fizzle out, firefighter Sasha and reluctant millionairess Abby find themselves turning to each other to strike a perfect match. (978-1-62639-999-0)

The Price of Cash by Ashley Bartlett. Cash Braddock is doing her best to keep her business afloat, stay out of jail, and avoid Detective Kallen. It's not working. (978-1-62639-708-8)

Under Her Wing by Ronica Black. At Angel's Wings Rescue, dogs are usually the ones saved, but when quiet Kassandra Haden meets outspoken owner Jayden Beaumont, the two stubborn women just might end up saving each other. (978-1-63555-077-1)

Underwater Vibes by Mickey Brent. When Hélène, a translator in Brussels, Belgium, meets Sylvie, a young Greek photographer and swim coach, unsettling feelings hijack Hélène's mind and body—even her poems. (978-1-63555-002-3)

A More Perfect Union by Carsen Taite. Major Zoey Granger and DC fixer Rook Daniels risk their reputations for a chance at true love while dealing with a scandal that threatens to rock the military. (978-1-62639-754-5)

Arrival by Gun Brooke. The spaceship *Pathfinder* reaches its passengers' new homeworld where danger lurks in the shadows while Pamas Seclan disembarks and finds unexpected love in young science genius Darmiya Do Voy. (978-1-62639-859-7)

Captain's Choice by VK Powell. Architect Kerstin Anthony's life is going to plan until Bennett Carlyle, the first girl she ever kissed, is assigned to her latest and most important project, a police district substation. (978-1-62639-997-6)

Falling Into Her by Erin Zak. Pam Phillips, widow at the age of forty, meets Kathryn Hawthorne, local Chicago celebrity, and it changes her life forever—in ways she hadn't even considered possible. (978-1-63555-092-4)

Hookin' Up by MJ Williamz. Will Leah get what she needs from casual hookups or will she see the love she desires right in front of her? (978-1-63555-051-1)

King of Thieves by Shea Godfrey. When art thief Casey Marinos meets bounty hunter Finnegan Starkweather, the crimes of the past just might set the stage for a payoff worth more than she ever dreamed possible. (978-1-63555-007-8)

Lucy's Chance by Jackie D. As a serial killer haunts the streets, Lucy tries to stitch up old wounds with her first love in the wake of a small town's rapid descent into chaos. (978-1-63555-027-6)

Right Here, Right Now by Georgia Beers. When Alicia Wright moves into the office next door to Lacey Chamberlain's accounting firm, Lacey is about to find out that sometimes the last person you want is exactly the person you need. (978-1-63555-154-9)

Strictly Need to Know by MB Austin. Covert operator Maji Rios will do whatever she must to complete her mission, but saving a gorgeous stranger from Russian mobsters was not in her plans. (978-1-63555-114-3)

Tailor-Made by Yolanda Wallace. Tailor Grace Henderson doesn't date clients, but when she meets gender-bending model Dakota Lane, she's tempted to throw all the rules out the window. (978-1-63555-081-8)

Time Will Tell by M. Ullrich. With the ability to time travel, Eva Caldwell will have to decide between having it all and erasing it all. (978-1-63555-088-7)

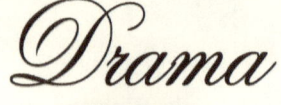